SUBMIT—A SCI-FI ALIEN WARRIOR ROMANCE

THE SKY CLAN OF THE TAORI #1

TANA STONE

BROADMOOR BOOKS

CHAPTER
ONE

Torst

"Any luck hunting females?"

"No, Kalesh," our first officer answered the Taori warrior who strode onto the command deck, a steel mesh sash across his bare chest denoting his elevated rank as kalesh on our sky ship.

"Then our mission continues." Kalesh Naz took his place on the raised platform and set his feet wide, his tail swishing behind him to a steady beat. Strands of silver glinted in his black hair, but the scruff on his cheek was as dark as it had been when we first took to the skies so many decades ago.

I glanced quickly at the other Taori warriors on the command deck, their majestic, silvery horns curling back from their ears as they stood at their own consoles. Like me, they had dark hair they wore long and interspersed with braids, dark ink curling down from their necks to cover almost every available bit of skin. Since we were on our sky ship, we didn't wear anything covering our chests, and our black, animal-skin pants hung low on our hips, blades hooked to the waistbands.

1

This was how the Immortal Army of the Taori preferred to fight. No uniforms. No insignia. Just the markings on our bodies that told the story of our people and our journey across the skies in pursuit of our enemy. Not that we'd encountered the Sythian swarm since we'd left the Drexian battleship.

That wasn't our current mission. Our mission was to find a cure for our Taori brother's mating fever. Barring a cure, we would settle for a hedonistic planet where he could indulge his growing compulsion. One problem with leaving your home world to chase down your enemy on a sky ship filled only with male Taori warriors was the lack of compatible females. We'd passed many planets with females who were both incompatible with us and unappealing. Some, like the Farfallians—with tentacles for arms and barbed suckers for mouths—had been terrifying.

"Any planets on long range scanners?" Kalesh Naz asked.

Skard glanced up from his navigational readings, the bone necklace swinging from his neck. "None that appear to be planets of hedonism, Kalesh."

The kalesh cursed and ran a hand along the curve of one of his silvery striped horns. "There must be houses of hedonism on one of the planets. The Drexians assured us this galaxy had plenty of options for warriors." He pivoted to first officer, Kaos, whose black hair was intricately braided on one side and whose chest was emblazoned with an open-mouthed skull that stretched from his shoulders to his hips. "How is Daik doing?"

Kaos grimaced at the mention of Daiken. "He's still sedated, but the symptoms are progressing. If he doesn't find a suitable mate soon, the madness will set in."

Rumbles passed through the warriors on deck. No one wished our Taori brother to go mad because the Quaibyn, the mating fever which usually only took place once every ten astro-years, had reoccurred without warning. The acceleration of the Taori curse had put us all on edge. If it could consume Daiken suddenly, the same could happen to any one of us—and we had no idea why.

I braced my hands on the cool steel of the console and locked my gaze on the numbers and symbols flashing in blue and red across the smooth gray surface. My tail twitched nervously behind me, betraying my growing anxiety as I swished a hand up to bring the readouts into the air, the colorful numbers now light projections hovering at eye level. As the sky ship's security chief, I was alarmed by the warnings even though I couldn't yet decipher what they meant.

I cleared my throat. "This has nothing to do with our search, but I'm picking up some unusual readings on long-range scanners."

"Dangerous?" Naz asked.

I eyed the odd readings. "I can't say yet. They don't seem to be stable."

"An energy fluctuation?" Ruun asked, as he walked onto the bridge and leapt down from the platform to join me at my console, his dark top knot of hair quivering. The science chief peered at my readouts, grunting with obvious displeasure. "Strange. The readings aren't stable or anything I've seen before."

Naz growled, his tail flicking quickly as he resumed pacing. "We don't have time to investigate." He cut his gaze to Ruun. "No matter how intriguing."

"Change course?" Skard asked, his fingers hovering over his navigational controls.

Naz gave a curt nod. "And continue to search for a pleasure planet."

"We could send out hails to any pleasure ships," Kaos said. "The Drexians did say there are a few independent madams in the skies."

"Do it," Naz told his first officer. "The faster we can aid Daiken, the faster we can join the hunt for the Sythians."

I shifted from one foot to the other, ignoring the nervous flutter in my gut as I glanced again at the readouts. Ruun was right. The readings were like nothing I'd seen before—both erratic and powerful. I wanted to be wrong, but my gut instinct had been honed over decades and as many galaxies. I'd led our sky ship into too many battles to push aside the tingle creeping up my spine, but I also knew our mission could not be delayed.

Murmuring a brief prayer to the gods of the ancients that the fluctuations wouldn't reach us and disrupt our systems, I held my breath as the ship's heading was changed. The view out the front of the command deck shifted, although the change in the blackness of space was minimal.

"I won't complain about stopping at a house of hedonism," Ruun said under his breath as he peered at the readouts hovering in the air in front of us.

I grinned at him. "You'll probably race Daiken to it."

Ruun laughed as he turned from me, the low rumbling sound making his body shake and his long silver pendant quiver as it swung from his neck. "If only the fever didn't give him extra speed and power. Speaking of our brother, I'd better check on him again."

I swallowed hard as I watched our science chief leave the command deck, my thoughts on Daiken and the Quaibyn that was consuming him. The longer he went without relief, the more manic he would become until his power and speed would be almost uncontrollable. Then I feared for any female who would encounter the frenzied and lust-fueled Taori.

Like all the Taori on our sky ship, I would greet a visit to pleasurers with nearly as much fervor as our ailing brother. It had been a long time since I'd thought about much but hunting Sythians or my own unquenchable desire for vengeance.

Female pleasurers would be a welcome change from a hunger for revenge that could never be sated.

"What kind of female have you wished to the gods for, Torst?"

I twisted my head to look at Skard standing at the console next to mine. The skin on his back was an intricately inked map of the stars we'd journeyed past since leaving home—fitting art for a navigation officer.

Before I could answer, he cursed under his breath. "Apologies. You know I share in the tears and sorrow for your fallen intended."

I shook off his apology even though the old memory made my throat tighten. The Taori female I'd been promised to as a mate had been gone for longer than we'd been traversing the skies in search of the Sythians—and we'd been on our journey for longer than some aliens' lifespans. "That life is all but a whisper. You know I don't begrudge myself release. This day, I wish for a female who isn't startled by our horns and tails."

Skard gave me a relieved grin as he glanced back at his own console. "These pleasurers won't be like the females on Alvaren."

I frowned as I remembered the horrified looks on the faces of the tiny, cloaked females who'd scurried away when they'd seen us stride bare chested off our ship. To us, our marked skin recorded our journey and our lore, but to some alien societies, it made us seem menacing—and our curled, pointed horns and long tails only added to their view that we were beasts. And they hadn't even seen us fully unclothed. More than one pleasurer had been open-mouthed to discover that our cocks boasted three crowns down the length of them. "I share in your hope, brother."

"As much as I honor you, Torst, I pray that is all we share when we finally locate a pleasure planet."

I choked back a laugh. "As do I, Skard." Then a jolt rocked the ship, knocking me off my feet. I caught myself by wrapping my tail around a nearby post before hitting the floor.

When I'd steadied myself enough to peer out the view screen, I was stunned. I'd expected to see a fleet of enemy vessels firing on us, Instead, there was a spiraling vortex of blue and white light.

"Where is the enemy?" Kalesh Naz bellowed as sirens blared. "Are they hiding from us? If so, let them come out and fight!"

I clutched the sides of my console for balance as I scanned the readings. It was the energy anomaly I'd detected earlier. "Impossible. We charted a course away from this."

Skard he let out a string of curses. "The anomaly shifted."

"Can we get away from it?" Naz paced like a caged animal across the raised platform of the command deck, his tail slashing through the air.

"Reverse thrusters are having no effect," Skard yelled back. "We're being pulled in."

I shot him a look. "If we keep trying to reverse from it, the ship might break apart."

His jaw was tight as he nodded. "Torst's right. Resisting the intense pull of this energy vortex might destroy the ship."

"So, we fly into it?" Naz asked.

I moved my hands across my console as columns of light rose to meet my fingers in an undulating pattern. "I'm rerouting power to the shields. That should give us some extra protection."

Naz looked from me to Skard and then set his mouth in a hard line. "Then take us in. May the ancients favor us on the other side."

Skard swung his head back to his console, extending his hands to steer the ship by the pulsing columns of blue. With a jolt, the ship ceased shaking as we flew toward the swirling light.

"Into the valley of death ride the Ten Thousand!" Kalesh Naz's voice boomed.

"We are the Taori!" I responded, along with the rest of the warriors on the command deck, our deep tones swelling like a towering wave as we rushed toward possible death. "We are the Immortals!"

I closed my eyes as the light became blinding, holding my breath as we were sucked into the vortex.

CHAPTER

TWO

Lia

I sat bolt upright in bed, my eyes searching the darkness as my heart raced. Had it been another nightmare? I inhaled slowly and pushed the blanket from me as I swung my feet off the bed, the coolness of the steel floor waking me even more.

My nightmares usually left me soaked with sweat and panting, but I was neither drenched in sweat nor gasping for breath. I also had no memories of the dreams that usually plagued my sleep, and no images of needles or sterile medical wards flashed through my brain. I braced my hands on the edge of the bed with my head bowed, willing myself not to relive a childhood teetering on the edge of death. Instead, I focused on breathing in and out, the sound as soothing in the dark as the gentle rumble of the ship beneath my feet.

If my dreams hadn't woken me, then why had I been jerked awake? A jolt rattled the floor, an almost instantaneous answer.

"Lights," I ordered, and my spartan quarters were illuminated. Blinking drowsily as I adjusted to the flickering overhead lights, I stood and tugged on a pair of murky-green, military issue pants. I jammed my feet into my boots and shrugged on a dark fleece jacket over my gray imperial insignia T-shirt before clipping a blaster to my waistband. Squinting into the warped mirror over my dresser, I sighed at my dark, upturned eyes that were puffy from lack of sleep. At least my straight, black hair looked okay as I tugged it up into a high ponytail, which was my default hairstyle.

I fought the urge to make my bed, telling myself that I wasn't subject to academy inspections anymore, and that I'd probably be crawling back in it soon. Still, I yanked the blanket up before heading into the corridor.

"You felt it, too?"

I turned at the sound of Carly's voice, giving my friend and fellow security force teammate a sleepy grin. "Turbulence again?"

She shrugged and flicked a hand through her tousled brown hair. "Must be, but the scraping sounds were new."

"Scraping?" I hadn't heard scraping, but maybe that had been the noise that had woken me.

"I could have sworn I heard metal against metal." Carly shook her head. "But I was also half asleep."

"Who's on duty for fifth watch?"

Carly scrunched her lips to one side as she thought. "Parker, I think."

I nodded at the mention of one of the few males on our team. He would have put the transport ship on alert if there was an issue, wouldn't he?

There was another jolt, and we both bumped the steel wall before we could steady ourselves. Then came the unmistakable sound of metal against metal.

"Shit." Carly looked at me with her brow wrinkled. "I didn't imagine that."

I shook my head, and we both pulled out our blasters. "That wasn't turbulence."

The sounds were emanating from the rear of the ship, but the science lab we were transporting was in the other direction. Our defensive unit had been assigned to protect imperial transports, and this particular run was taking a group of scientists and their research to a safer colony, so I felt torn about where to go. Should I go toward the sound or ensure that the lab was safe?

"Parker should be guarding the lab," Carly said, as if sensing my unspoken question. "We should check out the noise."

We assumed tactical stances as we moved swiftly along the corridor, peeking down offshoot hallways before closing in on the compact hangar bay. There had been no more shaking since we'd started closing in on the location, but the ship was unusually quiet, even for the deserted fifth watch, when most of the crew and researchers were sleeping.

My heart had resumed its steady drumbeat, and my hands were steady as I held my blaster in front of me. I'd been trained well, even if I hadn't been in many combat situations. Serving as security for transports wasn't considered combat duty, and I couldn't help thinking that my small stature had something to do with me landing on a team that was unlikely to see action.

Their mistake, I thought, gripping my blaster tighter. I might not be as tall or broad as a man, but I'd gotten top marks at the academy in marksmanship and strategy. I was a crack shot, and I wasn't afraid to take out anyone as long as I didn't have to do it in hand-to-hand combat.

I brushed off this thought and concentrated on the mission at hand, my fingers tingling in anticipation.

Carly cut her gaze to me, her mouth curving into a half grin.

"This is probably a loose steel drum rolling around the hangar bay."

She was right. We were in unclaimed space. There were no sirens going off. There was no concrete indication of an incursion. Even so, a shiver went down my spine as we approached the entrance to the hangar bay.

"On my mark?" Carly whispered.

I gave her a single nod before she moved inside, and I followed behind her. She fired so quickly that I barely had a chance to react before her blaster was flying from her hand, and she went rigid beside me. I registered Parker lying sprawled on the gray floor, a dark pool expanding around his head, but my finger froze before I could squeeze the trigger and fire at the creatures standing behind him.

Despite being immobilized, my upper lip curled at the sight of the motley crew of aliens. Hettite slavers.

I shifted my gaze to the ship that was attached to ours, a gaping hole cut into the steel hull of the transport vessel I'd been tasked to protect. How had the captain of the ship not noticed we were being boarded? I glanced at Parker again, my stomach churning at the sight of his lifeless body. He'd obviously come to investigate and been killed for his trouble. So why weren't the pirates killing us?

A hulking alien with dark purple skin and yellowed tusks stepped forward, his rheumy eyes raking over Carly and me. "These will fetch a nice price."

Fear iced my skin. I'd rather be killed than sold into slavery.

"You should kill us," Carly gritted.

The alien laughed, his broad belly shaking. "They don't pay for dead females." He swung his head to his crew. "Gather any more on the ship. Kill the males."

As the ragged crew barreled past us, I struggled against the energy field holding me in place, straining hard enough that I was able to move my finger and fire my blaster. The beam went wide, missing the tusked alien I'd been hoping to hit.

He let out a guttural growl as he stomped toward me. "That was a mistake, human." Then he hit me over the head with his thick fist. Pain exploded across my skull, and Carly's screams were the last thing I heard.

THREE

Torst

My head ached as I pulled myself up to a sitting position. The alarms no longer wailed, but my ears rang over the sounds of groaning around me. As the command deck came into focus, I saw that I wasn't the only Taori who'd been knocked off his feet when we were pulled into the energy vortex. Warriors were sprawled on the steel floor, some hoisting themselves up and others still prone.

Naz leapt down from the top of the command platform and landed in a crouch, a trickle of blood trailing from his lip. "Report!"

"We've cleared the anomaly." Skard shook his head as if trying to dislodge his own horns.

I peered at the view screen. As our navigation officer said, we were no longer looking into a bright, swirling cone of light. The light was gone and now we were motionless in space—a blue-gray planet surrounded by three moons in front of us.

Naz swiped at the blood on his lip. "Where are we?"

Skard cocked his head as he looked down at his console.

"The readouts aren't clear, but we seem to be a considerable distance from where we started."

"Considerable?" our kalesh asked.

Skard's expression darkened as he nodded. "We aren't in the same galaxy."

The command deck went silent as we all absorbed this, and the old knot in my gut returned. How had the vortex taken us so far?

"So, a wormhole," Naz said.

Skard didn't look up as his frown deepened. "The emissions weren't entirely consistent with a wormhole. At least, not a standard wormhole."

Naz strode toward Skard. "Even if it was an anomalous wormhole, we must be able to use it to return to our initial point."

Skard looked up at the kalesh with a tormented expression. "The vortex, or anomolous wormhole, is gone."

Naz stared at the warrior for a beat. "Impossible." He glanced at the readings himself then rubbed a hand over his eyes. "We'll wait for it to reappear. It would take us years to make up the distance we lost, and who knows if there are any pleasure ships or planets near our current location. Daiken doesn't have years."

Kaos rushed onto the command deck breathing heavily. "Was that an attack?"

"An anomalous wormhole," Skard answered when the kalesh gave him a pointed look.

The first officer's shoulders sagged as he looked at the view of space. "What planet is that?"

Skard's brow furrowed. "The star chart says it's an M-class planet called Xulon, with three inhabitable moons."

"Are they capable of space flight?" I asked Skard, my mind

whirring as I assessed the chances the planet would be hostile to a ship suddenly popping into the space above them.

"We have virtually no information about this part of space."

I attempted to scan the planet's surface with long range sensors, but our instruments weren't responding like they usually did. "I don't detect radiation that would indicate weapons of significant destructive force, but our sensors might have been affected when we were pulled through the wormhole."

"That would explain my readouts." Skard scowled at his console.

Naz rocked back on his heels, his gaze not leaving the view screen. "Let's run a ship-wide diagnostic to assess any damage."

Ruun strode onto the command deck, his gaze quickly taking in the change in view. He joined me at my console without a word, peering at the readings scrolling down the smooth surface. "That explains it."

"Explains what?" Kaos asked.

"If the energy vortex was a wormhole, then it explains why the event affected Daiken." Before anyone could ask, he took a quick breath. "The fever accelerated after we were pulled through."

Our kalesh growled low, fisting his hands by his side. "Is it still curable?"

Ruun's face twisted briefly as if he was in pain. "I don't know. We increased his sedation, but he needs relief that drugs can't provide. No chance a pleasure ship was pulled through with us?"

I shook my head. My scans had revealed no other ships in our vicinity.

Ruun leaned closer to my console, cocking his head to one side. "This doesn't make sense." He held his hands above the dark, glossy surface, making more noises of disapproval as columns of blue light rose and fell with each flick of his fingertips.

Kalesh Naz pivoted to face us. "What does my science chief know that we don't?"

Ruun lifted his head, his jaw clenched, then glanced back down and shook his head. "I believe I know why our readings are off, and our systems are out of alignment." He straightened and drew in a long breath as he faced our kalesh. "I suspect the wormhole was temporal."

Everyone stared at Ruun as the word sank in.

"Do you mean we've traveled through time, as well as through space?" our first officer asked, his voice cutting through the hush of the command deck.

"If my calculations are correct, we were thrown five hundred astro-years forward in time."

"Sons of the cursed ones," I said under my breath. Five hundred? That meant that all our Taori brothers who'd been chasing after the Sythian swarm were gone, along with our families back on the Taori home world. Even though our lives spanned over two hundred astro-years, not even our elders had reached five hundred.

Our kalesh cleared his throat. "If this is true, and the temporal energy sped up our Taori brother's mating fever, is there any chance that it will trigger the fever in the rest of us?"

Ruun huffed out a breath. "I have no way of knowing for sure, but we should be prepared."

My knees wobbled as I absorbed all this. We were in a distant galaxy hundreds of astro-years from our own time, the wormhole that had brought us here had vanished, and we could all be struck down with mating fever at any time. Even for a species used to battling seemingly insurmountable odds, this was soul crushing.

"Now is not the time to falter in our courage," Naz said, his voice booming, as though he knew what the rest of us were thinking. "Now is the time to draw on the wisdom of our people and the travails of our travels. This is not where our journey ends. Not today. We are the Immortal Army of the Taori!"

The force and certainty of his words strengthened me. I squared my shoulders and grunted my agreement, along with the rest of the warriors on the command deck. Then I dropped my gaze to my console, and fear gripped my heart. I glanced at the view screen, unable to believe what was bursting in red streaks from the surface of the planet.

"Incoming missiles!" I managed to yell, before the first hit tore into the ship.

FOUR

Lia

"Lia!" The voice was faint, but the tone was urgent enough that I forced my eyes to open. Carly's face swam into focus as I groaned from the ache in my head. I attempted to lift my hands to touch my forehead, but they were bound with metal ties that bit into my wrists.

"Don't try to move too much," another voice cautioned. "That bruise on your noggin looks bad."

I shifted my gaze to Jasmine, whose heavily lashed, brown eyes were wide with concern. Why was she here? The last thing I remembered was being with Carly. Then I remembered where we'd been and what we'd been doing, and I blinked rapidly, swiveling my gaze around the cramped cell with a humming energy field extending across the one open side. "Where are we?"

"The Hettite slave ship," Carly said. "Every woman from the transport is here."

I slowly craned my neck to take in the other women sitting along the dank walls. I didn't know the scientists well, but I recognized two of them from my guard shifts. The other woman huddled in the shadowy corner of the cell was a mystery. I inclined my head toward the female with short, pink hair and nudged Carly. "Who's that?"

"I don't know anything about her," Carly said under her breath. "Only that the empire paid for her passage to the colony."

I wasn't sure if she was human or not, but she looked as scared as the rest of us. Before I could ask any more questions, the door to the brig opened.

The purple-skinned alien lumbered inside, and a grin spilt his grotesque face when he saw me. "You made it. For a while, I thought I'd hit you too hard. You humans are a fragile species." He grimaced, an expression that didn't look any better on him than a smile. "It's a mystery why the Xulon prefer you. Maybe because you're easier to fight and fuck?"

I bristled at this and sensed both Carly and Jasmine tense as well. I decided not to respond, since my head throbbed, and I didn't relish being silenced again.

"Get up," the slaver ordered, flicking a meaty hand at us.

Carly helped me stand, even though her hands were also bound, and we stood side by side. The only person who didn't make a move to rise was the woman slumped over in the corner.

The alien let out a menacing rumble. "You! Lycithian!"

The female twisted her neck to pin the alien slaver with silver eyes that glimmered. "I'm not Lycithian," she muttered darkly. "If I were, I'd have shapeshifted into a creature who could rip off your head."

The slaver leaned in, cocking his head to one side. "What?"

She stood, not answering him but moving next to the rest of us. She might not have been a Lycithian shapeshifter, but she wasn't human. I wondered what kind of alien the empire was transporting so secretly.

The purple-skinned alien pulled a battered device from his pocket and roughly jabbed at it until the holographic image of a tall, cloaked creature flickered to life in front of us. Its hands were clasped together so that the pale fabric of the cloak covered them entirely.

"The latest shipment for your review, Praetor."

The cloaked alien tipped his head back to reveal red skin pulled tight over a long-boned face. "They aren't all human?"

The slaver shifted his bare feet. "Almost all are human, like you wanted."

Why did this cloaked alien want human women so badly? I glanced at Carly and then at Jasmine. Both of my friends were scowling at the aliens appraising us.

"They are acceptable," the cloaked alien said, turning his head and nodding sharply before his image flickered into nothingness.

"Acceptable for what?" I asked.

"If you just sold us off as sex slaves, your buyers are going to be pretty disappointed," Carly said, advancing toward the energy barrier. "We'd all rather die first."

The alien snorted out a laugh. "Some of you will have that chance."

"What the fuck?" Jasmine mouthed to me.

"You don't know about Xulon, do you?" Our alien captor's watery eyes sparkled with barely contained glee. When no one responded, he continued. "They don't like to interact with other planets, but they like to entertain themselves."

"What the hell does that mean?" Carly asked.

The slaver twitched one beefy shoulder. "They've got wealth from all their mining, but now their planet is overcrowded and polluted. Rich Xulonians require other creatures to provide entertainment and escape."

Carly folded her arms over her chest. "So, we're being sold to amuse the privileged on some alien planet?"

Another guttural laugh from the slaver. "You won't ever see the planet. You'll be on one of their moons."

I fought back a shiver, noticing for the first time that my fleece was gone, and I wore only my imperial T-shirt and pants. "What's on the moons?"

"Whatever the directors create that can entertain. The Xulonians pay well to be entertained on their moons." He grinned coldly. "Too bad for you that entertainment requires plenty of expendables."

"We're expendables?"

"They need someone to hunt and to watch in battle," he licked his cracked lips, "and to watch mate."

My stomach lurched, and I tasted bile in the back of my throat. What kind of messed up entertainment was this?

"You can't do this," one of the scientists said, her voice trembling. "We work for the empire."

"The empire has no power here. The Xulonians don't allow contact with other worlds, and they have the defensive systems to back up their isolation." He sneered. "Be grateful you're female. All the males on your ships had their throats slit. At least you have a chance to survive." His sneer morphed into a leer. "Especially those of you chosen for the lust moon. There are no blood games there, although rumor has it the male aliens they bring to the moon are not easily satisfied."

Then he lumbered from the room, his cruel laugh echoing down the hall, while we all stood with our mouths open.

Carly turned around to face us, locking eyes with each female in turn. "After we escape, we're killing that asshole. Got it?"

CHAPTER
FIVE

Torst

My roar tore across the command deck just before the blast knocked me off my feet. Pain shot through my knees as I landed hard on the steel floor, and I tasted blood as my teeth slammed together and bit the side of my tongue. Swallowing the metallic tang of my own blood, I hoisted myself to my feet and clutched the sides of my standing console.

More arcs of red were erupting from the surface of the planet Xulon and racing toward our Taori battleship. I quickly scanned our shield's power, my heart sinking when I saw the dismal readings. How had the missile torn through our defenses and done so much damage? Our ship was equipped with cutting-edge shielding, but our systems were faltering after only a single strike.

Another hit made the command deck pitch hard to one side, but I managed to stay upright. Sirens wailed as crimson lights flashed overhead, making the horns of the Taori warrior beside me appear red instead of their usual silvery gray as he struggled to stand. I grabbed him by the elbow and heaved him to a standing position.

"Damage report." Kalesh Naz's voice cut through the sirens and cacophony of voices. He stood with his arms and legs braced wide, the pulsing, red light illuminating the dark marks covering his bare chest beneath the steel mesh. His tail coiled around an iron beam to keep him steady, and his jaw was tight.

"Hull breaches on all decks." I swallowed more blood, but the coppery taste was overpowered by the acrid scent of smoke filling the command deck. "Fires on decks five and six where the missile impacted. Automatic fire suppression activated."

Our kalesh grunted. "Were we not flying beyond the veil? How did any enemy target us?"

I managed to hold my palm over the surface of my console, raising it slightly until glowing blue numbers and symbols appeared in the air. "The wormhole we were sucked through knocked out our stealth capabilities. We are no longer beyond the veil of sight."

Naz uttered an ancient Taori curse. "Even so, what kind of missile could rip through our shields as if they were nothing?"

Kaos kept his eyes trained on the surface of planet Xulon. "A missile that's had five hundred astro-years of technological advancement."

The knot in my stomach tightened, and my gaze flicked to Ruun, whose face was like stone. My mind reeled from the knowledge that the energy field we'd been sucked through while in pursuit of the Sythian swarm had been a wormhole that had deposited us in an entirely different galaxy. The fact that we were also five hundred astro-years in the future was almost too much to comprehend.

Temporal wormholes were a myth, whispered about in

murky corners. They'd never been witnessed or experienced. Not by anyone who'd returned to tell the tale.

Ruun's expression was dark as he swayed from the residual impact of the missile strikes and fingered the silver pendant hanging from his neck. "I'm afraid there is truth in Kaos's words. We are no longer in possession of the most sophisticated weaponry in the universe. To the planet Xulon, we must appear as a relic."

"Then why bother destroying us?" our kalesh asked, fury radiating from him. "We posed no threat and made no moves of hostility."

"We know nothing of this galaxy or planet or species." Kaos made his way to stand next to Kalesh Naz. "For all we know, they are warmongers who attack any ship that wanders into their territory."

Naz curled his hands into fists. "Hail the planet. Tell them we bring no battle to their doorstep today and will gladly leave their space."

"No answer, Kalesh," a warrior called out after a few moments.

I raised and lowered my hands above the cracked surface of my console, attempting to reroute power to our shields even though the beams of light extending to meet my hands flickered weakly. I couldn't pull power from the fields containing the hull breaches, but I could reduce nonessential power to the minimum. "I'm fortifying our shielding. Should we return fire, Kalesh?"

"And provoke the spirit of hate that flows like blood down a slick blade?" Naz strode over to me, peering at the undulating columns of blue light connecting the console to my hands and grunting more. "We can't withstand many more hits."

"No, we can't. The whisper of death grows louder, Kalesh."

As security chief, making that admission was painful. It was my duty to defend the ship and all my Taori brothers, but I was outmatched by the enemy's technology. All I could do was shore up defenses until the ship finally tore apart at its iron seams. For a Taori warrior like me who'd dedicated his life to seeking vengeance on the Sythian swarm that had ravaged our planet and torn my life asunder, this was a bitter draught to swallow.

Kalesh Naz drew himself up to his full and impressive height. "We are the Immortal Army of the Taori. We shall not be defeated today."

His courage stirred a fire within me, and I threw back my shoulders. The Taori had been an invincible force for generations, battling across the brutal terrain of our home world, and then taking our fight to the skies as we chased down the Sythian swarm that raged across the galaxy. I felt a certainty hardening inside me. This would not be our end. "Your orders, Kalesh?"

He pivoted to face the command deck warriors as another hit rattled the floor beneath us. "Into the valley of death ride the Ten Thousand."

My throat tightened at the familiar refrain that had led us into battle since ancient days. Like the other warriors on the command deck, I squared my shoulders and bellowed my response. "We are the Taori! We are Immortal!"

The floors shook from our chant, the shuddering of the hull ceasing for a few beats.

"We are called the Immortals because of illusion," Kalesh Naz continued. "Illusion has always been a part of our power, as has our connection to the realm beyond the veil. Today, we harness the power of illusion to restore our Ten Thousand."

I glanced at the dropping shield strength, hoping our

kalesh's strategy included a way to keep our ship from being blown to shards. We had little time before our enemy would prevail.

"There is power in survival," Kalesh Naz continued, "even though there is honor in a well-fought death. In this time and in this battle, we will scatter ourselves across the battlefield like stars scattered across the sky—so we can reform and defeat our enemy when he least expects it."

My spine tingled with trepidation as I unwound his words. Abandon ship?

Kaos comprehended his meaning at the same time I did. He locked his gaze on mine. "Maximum strength to our shielding and set up defensive fire to distract from our mission." Then he swept his gaze across the remaining warriors at their posts. "The shuttles are too easy to target with missiles. To the escape pods."

There was a pause as the command deck warriors absorbed this, but a bone rattling hit on our ship jolted everyone into action. I did as our first officer instructed, quickly activating a delayed pattern of automatic laser fire that I hoped would distract our attackers long enough for our escape pods to make it to safety.

I hurried off the command deck behind my Taori brothers, the pounding of our boots echoing through the corridors and swirling with the undulating sirens and pained screams coming from the bowels of the ship. Not every Taori would make it to an escape pod, and the thought of our casualties made my stomach roil. I was no stranger to battle or death, but I mourned for those who would not receive the Taori death rites to take them to the shadowlands.

After thundering down a series of stairs, I spotted Kaos waving warriors toward rows of shiny, cylindrical pods. I instinctively glanced over my shoulder, even though the command deck was now many decks away. "The Kalesh?"

A muscle ticked in our first officer's jaw. "He insisted on being the last warrior off the ship."

I gave Kaos a single nod, bile sharp in my throat at the thought of our leader's courage.

"Our duty to our kalesh is to survive and follow his orders," he continued. "We will find each other and reemerge more powerful than before, as the Immortal Army has always done."

I touched a hand to my horns, the grooves comforting in their familiarity before repeating the mantra. "We are the Immortals."

"And the Immortals are Taori," Ruun finished for me, thumping a hand on my shoulder as he passed.

I lifted a brow in question at the science chief.

"I must get our brother, Daiken," he said, answering what I hadn't even asked. "I'm afraid the sedation we gave him after coming through the temporal wormhole might make him difficult to transfer into a pod."

My mind went to the Taori who was suffering from mating fever. If the temporal shift had exacerbated his symptoms, the rapidly progressing fever put him in even graver danger. I feared what would happen to the warrior once he was sent out in an escape pod by himself. There was no guarantee he'd land in the same place as any of the medical crew. Then again, there was a chance that none of our escape pods would make it past the volley of enemy missiles.

A siren's blare punctuated the air, followed by a robotic voice. "Shielding failing. Catastrophic hull breaches imminent."

Ruun broke into a run, and Kaos pulled me roughly toward him and an empty pod. "I will see you on the other side, Torst."

There was no time to reply as he shoved me into the pod

and pressed the button to seal it. I caught a glimpse of Naz joining Kaos in loading the last pods as I fumbled with the safety straps and adjusted myself in the standing seat that reclined slightly. Air flowed from above as the pod shifted into the launch tube, the wailing sirens from the battleship muffled as the hatch closed.

This was insanity, I thought. The chances that we'd all land someplace safe—or land at all—were minuscule. The idea that we'd be able to find each other again and regroup into the Immortals, as our ancestors had done, was even more impossible. But impossible was not something the Taori believed in, even though every fiber of my being told me that I would never see my kinsmen again.

With a deafening roar, my escape pod rocketed through the metal tube and burst into space. My breath caught in my throat as I was shot through the air that was thick with laser fire from our ship and incoming missiles from the enemy planet. The red beams arched above me, slashing the black sky like blood, as my trajectory spun me toward the nearby moons, which appeared serene compared to the battle raging above them.

I attempted to track the other pods emerging from our battleship—streaks of silver crisscrossing the red ones—and determine if any were falling near me, but the paths seemed scattered and wide-ranging. Before I could lock onto any neighboring pods, our battleship was hit by another missile and exploded.

I gasped as the ship that had been my home was torn to bits, chunks of the hull spiraling through the air. My own escape pod shuddered from the blast, and as it started to lose control and spin toward the surface of one of the Xulon moons covered in swirling pastel clouds, I squeezed my eyes tight and muttered a lament for all my Taori brothers who would be taken to the shadowland.

"I hold the memory of your souls in mine until we meet on the other side of the eternal veil."

Then I said a quick Taori lament for myself before the uncontrolled speed of my descent rendered me blissfully unconscious.

CHAPTER
SIX

Lia

When I opened my eyes, sunlight slatted through a canopy of blue and purple leaves overhead. My temples throbbed, but then I remembered that was from before. I groaned as I sat up, recalling being hit on the head by the Hettite slaver.

Shuddering at the thought of the creature with tusks coming from his face and beady, yellow eyes, I touched a hand to the bump on my head, realizing at the same time that my hands had been freed. At least there was no blood, although the throbbing pain wasn't much better.

As a member of the imperial security force assigned to keep the transport ship safe, shame washed over me at the thought of how easily the slavers had gotten on board our ship and massacred our crew. All except the females, I thought, wincing at the memory of one of my male colleagues lying dead on the floor of the hangar bay.

"Maybe he was the lucky one," I muttered to myself as I peered around the thick jungle. It seemed habitable, and I could breathe, even if the air was thick and hazy as pale pink motes drifted up, only to get caught on broad purple fronds and feathery branches. Iridescent and virtually transparent organisms that reminded me of floating jellyfish propelled themselves through the air, bumping into the dense foliage and spinning off in different directions.

If what the alien who'd purchased us said was true, I was on one of the planet Xulon's special moons—Moorla moons— where the wealthy residents of the overpopulated and polluted planet were entertained and indulged.

"It doesn't seem all that indulgent," I muttered, as I sat up. Then I remembered another thing the slaver had said—not all the moons were luxurious experiences. Some moons were used for hunting and others for some sort of games or races.

I stilled my heavy breathing to listen. If this was a racing moon, I didn't hear any speed pods. My pulse tripped nervously. The quiet of the jungle—interrupted only by the occasional cawing of a bird or rustle of the leaves—was unsettling. I had no clue which moon I was on, and no idea if I should be hiding or running.

For a moment, I wondered if I'd imagined the whole thing. The idea of moons created for nothing but entertainment of the privileged was so last millennia. Then again, no one knew much about the xenophobic Xulonians, so something twisted and antiquated wasn't impossible from a society that had eschewed contact with other species and the empire.

The empire! My pulse spiked. Surely, they'd send a fleet after us when they realized our transport was missing. *If* they realized we'd been ambushed and abducted. My hope deflated.

The Hettite slavers weren't known for leaving much evidence behind. For all I knew, they'd destroyed our transport completely, leaving no trace that they were responsible or where they'd taken us.

That meant I couldn't count on a rescue. I got to my feet and swept my gaze around me, searching for any indication of where I was, and what I could expect. Aside from unusually colored fauna and willowy trees that stretched into the sky, there was nothing. I couldn't even tell from the thick, milky pink atmosphere if I was close to the planet Xulon or any of the other moons.

"I guess it's just me." I brushed off my pants, feeling for my blaster in the back waistband of my pants but not being surprised it was gone. "Or they spread us over the surface of the moon."

The possibility that my friends and fellow security officers Carly and Jasmine might be somewhere on the same moon heartened me. We'd worked together on quite a few transport missions now, and I'd learned to trust them. Being stranded on an alien moon wouldn't be so bad if I could find one of them.

"Hello?"

The tentative female voice didn't belong to one of my fellow security force officers. I instinctively reached for a weapon, cursing when I remembered I had none. Still, the voice wasn't entirely unfamiliar, and I stepped toward it. "Identify yourself."

"It's Valeria, Val. Everyone calls me Val."

I brushed aside a large, purple frond and shoved one of the clear, floating creatures from my face. One of the scientists from the transport was huddled behind a bush with feathery leaves sending spiraling bits of fluff into the air every time she moved. "You're from the lab."

She straightened and brushed her dark, wavy hair off her shoulder. "And you're part of the security detail."

"Lia." It felt funny to be introducing myself to someone I'd been sharing a ship with for the past few days, but I hadn't bothered to learn the names of the individuals we were transporting, and I doubted she'd learned mine.

"Do you know where we are?" Val asked, rubbing her own temples, and making me think we'd been drugged before being dumped onto the surface of the moon. It would explain why my head felt so heavy and my movements so sluggish.

"If we believe the asshole who bought us, we're on one of their weird moons."

Her eyes went wide. "You mean there are rich aliens out there right now, watching us?"

I swiveled my own head at this, searching for cameras in trees or hovering drones. I'd never thought that we might be monitored, but it stood to reason that they had some way to track us or monitor their own citizens. Then I remembered the disgusting slaver saying something about the Xulonians watching others mate on the lust moon. Cool fear danced across my skin. "I don't know. I haven't been able to figure out which of the moons this is yet."

Val rubbed the front of her brown pants nervously. "Do we even know how many different kinds there are?"

"Not really," I admitted. "I only know that hunting and racing are involved on at least one."

"And fucking," Val said darkly, as her gaze darted around us.

I didn't want to think about that. It wasn't like I was a prude or anything, but it had been a while since I'd hooked up with a guy, and I didn't feel like getting back into practice while being watched by some creepy aliens. I might prefer to be hunted.

Val squared her shoulders and huffed out a breath. "We need a plan. Or I should say, I need a plan. I'm a science nerd. I don't do well when I don't have an agenda."

As a member of the security team, I should be taking the lead. At least when it came to things like safety and staying alive. It also occurred to me that Val was still part of the cargo I was tasked to transport safely. It was my job to help her survive this.

For a moment, my mother's warnings rushed into my head. She'd never believed I was cut out for the military academy, much less being a security officer. If she'd had her way, I'd be safe and sound back on Lexirria, doing something that involved paperwork and a desk and nothing remotely dangerous or exciting. But after a childhood spent sick and fussed over, safe was the last thing I'd wanted.

Be careful what you wish for, I told myself, forcing my mother's doubts from my mind and remembering that even though I might not have been the strongest or biggest cadet to graduate from the academy, I did make it through—and I was trained for something like this. I glanced around the strange, shimmery jungle. Whatever this was.

"The first thing we should do is find shelter," I said, with more authority than I felt. "I'm not sure when night falls around here, or if there are any wild animals aside from these floaty things, but we don't want to be exposed any more than we need to be. Then we can figure out water and food."

"We won't last long without water." Val touched a hand to a nearby leaf that was the size of her hand. "But the foliage is damp, so I'm sure we can collect water from that, if we can't find a fresh source. Not that botany is my specialty."

I nodded, grateful for the first time that I was stranded with one of the scientists. I would have preferred to be with Carly or Jasmine, especially since they were both tougher and more experienced than me, but they wouldn't know how to collect water from trees, so maybe I'd lucked out after all.

"Once we lock in what we need for survival, we can figure

out weapons," I said, more to myself than to Val.

"It's so quiet. Do you really think this could be one of the dangerous moons?"

I didn't tell her that I thought they were all dangerous, if you were one of the expendable slaves used for the Xulonians' amusement. Instead, I picked a direction, walking as gingerly as possible through the thick undergrowth. "I have no idea. If you were an alien creating entertainment for other privileged aliens, why would you use a jungle?"

Val was quiet for a while, as she followed behind me. If she had any thoughts on what would be fun about a jungle so hot and humid that sweat was trailing down my back and beading on my upper lip, she didn't say. Even with my hair up a ponytail, damp tendrils clung stubbornly to my neck.

When she clutched my arm, I jumped.

"Do you hear that?" she whispered.

I was about to snap that I didn't hear a thing and she'd scared me half to death, but then I heard it—the faint rush of water. I turned to her and grinned. "It sounds like a stream."

"That's one of the things checked off our list." She let out a breath. "Plus, I don't have to try to get water from leaves. That was going to be tedious, and Harper is better at anything like that."

I assumed Harper was one of the other female scientists we'd been transporting, but I didn't get a chance to ask her, before something whizzed between us, narrowing missing hitting my nose. I swung my head to look at the shiny arrow that had lodged itself in the tree behind us. Suddenly, I knew exactly which of the moons we were on.

Val gasped. "We're being hunted."

I grabbed her hand and pulled her down with me, as I started to race through the jungle and more arrows zipped over our heads.

CHAPTER
SEVEN

Torst

Acrid smoke filled my lungs, forcing a rough cough from my lips. I jerked awake, my eyes stinging from the bitter air and my chest constricting in pain. My view was hindered by the smoke, but I could tell I wasn't hurtling through space. The escape pod was still, no longer being buffeted by the explosion of the Taori battleship and propelled faster toward the alien moon.

The sky ship. I bit down on my lower lip to keep a roar from escaping as I thought of my ship exploding—the ship that had been my home for longer than I'd even lived on Taor. I swallowed the taste of blood on my lips and pressed my palms to the murky window of the pod, careful not to suck in more smoke. After attempting to wipe the glass clean, I realized the smoke was outside the pod as well as inside.

"Curse of the goddess, I'm on fire." I felt around the inside of the pod until I found the emergency latch and popped it open.

The pod door released, and after I unhooked my safety straps, I stumbled forward and away from the smoking cylinder.

Gasping and coughing, I staggered far enough away from the scorched pod that I was no longer inhaling bitter air, even though the moon's heavy, moist atmosphere wasn't refreshing. I braced my hands on my knees, as I bent over and heaved in deep breaths.

Once I could breathe easily again, I peered around. "What is this place?"

I hadn't seen much as I'd approached the moon. Nothing but thick atmosphere, and no indication of the lush jungle beneath the pale pink swirling clouds. Then I'd lost consciousness and blacked out, missing the part where the pod's chute had deployed, and I'd flown through the atmosphere so fast my vessel had apparently caught on fire, and I'd crashed through the thick vegetation. Tipping my head back, I could track my pod's path through the trees by the broken branches. The chute hadn't slowed me much, but the jungle had.

"At least this wasn't an ice or water planet," I said to myself. "That landing wouldn't have been broken by anything."

The jungle reminded me of a thickly forested planet we'd visited once on our long journey, although the plants here were curious shades of blue and purple, and some of the leaves appeared almost diaphanous. Small, pink puffs of dust floated through the air and stuck to my skin, disintegrating when I swiped at them. I didn't spot any creatures in the trees, which boasted trunks thinner than my forearms, but perhaps my fiery arrival had scared them away.

Straightening, I took another strategic sweep of my surroundings, my training as security chief kicking in. I felt for the serrated blade hooked to my waist, as I appraised any possible threats. Was this moon populated? It was habitable, but this part of it appeared primitive—much more primitive than the planet that fired the deadly weapons at us.

Although I heard nothing but some distant chirping, I couldn't be sure there weren't violent and aggressive aliens somewhere on the moon. The planet Xulon had ignored our hails and brutally attacked our ship without provocation. I had to assume that if there was anyone on this moon, they were armed and deadly.

Then a thought occurred to me, and my pulse fluttered with excitement. At least one of the other escape pods must have made it to the surface like I did. Even though we all went in different directions, I'd seen other pods around me before the explosion. If they'd also crashed onto this moon, maybe they'd come in hot and fast too.

I craned my neck to search for other trails of smoke curling into the air, but the trees were too tall and too close together. I needed to find a clearing so I could get a better view.

I also needed to get away from the smoke pouring from my own pod and alerting anyone to my presence. Pulling my blade from my waist, I hacked my way through the dangling vines, flinching when a few seemed to reach for me and curl around my wrists and tail. When a delicate length of vine encircled one of my horns, I swept my blade over my head and sliced at the hanging blue tendril.

Was it my imagination or were the vines moving of their own accord? I pivoted in place, eyeing the jungle, but it was still and quiet. I touched my fingers to my horn and yanked off the remaining vine. I scoffed at myself. The jungle wasn't alive. I rubbed my horn, and the sensitive ridges calmed me. Maybe the impact of the crash had addled my mind, I thought. Or perhaps I'd inhaled too much smoke. Either could make me imagine things.

I grunted roughly. I didn't have time to indulge this weakness. I needed to find any other Taori who might have crashed on the moon, and then we needed to figure out how to rejoin our fellow warriors. I tried to push aside the questions that flooded my brain, but it was impossible. Even if we got all our warriors back together, we had no battleship. How were we supposed to assemble the Immortal Army of the Taori with no ship?

A low growl startled me, and I froze in place. I held my breath as I slowly swiveled my head. When it came again, I didn't need to turn. I put a hand to my bare chest, my fingers splayed across the dark ink that told of my victories in battle. The deep rumbling emanated from within me.

My heart thumped so loudly I was afraid it might give me away if there was anyone around to hear me. I hadn't intended to growl. I hadn't known I was growling. It had sprung from within me like a beast unleashed.

I curled the hand pressed to my chest into a tight fist, struggling to regain control and comprehend what had just happened. This was not the first time I'd experienced uncontrollable growling, but I knew it was only the first sign of what was to come. I closed my eyes, the hot stirrings within me unmistakable.

First would come the growling and heightened sense of smell. Then would come the racing heart and scorching skin that would feel as if I was being consumed by fire. Next would come the predatory stalking that could only be stopped by capturing my prey. The right prey. A compatible female I could mate with until the grip of the fever was burned away—and until the swollen clench of my cock released her.

I scraped a hand through my hair, my nails biting into my scalp. I'd heard Ruun's warning on the ship. The temporal wormhole had accelerated Daiken's mating fever, which meant that it could affect the rest of us as well. I just hadn't thought it would take effect so soon.

"This is the last thing I need." I ground out the words as I fought off the primal urge to release another growl. I was stranded on an alien moon that probably contained no compatible females. There was no way for me to quench the Taori mating fever that would soon consume me. And now that I wasn't on our ship, there was no way to slow the process with sedation. If I didn't find a way off the moon, the fever would eventually drive me mad. I shivered and shook my head roughly as I thought about my fate if the affliction wasn't treated or sated. I could not let *that* happen.

I barreled forward through the jungle, brushing aside diaphanous floating creatures resembling amoebas with tentacles, as I resumed my search for other stranded Taori. If I was being struck down by the fever, I might not be the only one. If the alien moons were now populated with Taori warriors in the throes of the Quaibyn, then I no longer feared the Xulon. No matter what their weaponry, they were no longer the deadliest creatures.

Fire bubbled deep within my core, sending hot tingles up my spine. "They have no idea what they've unleashed."

CHAPTER
EIGHT

Lia

My back and calves screamed in pain as we ran hunched over through the jungle. I used both hands to swat away the encroaching vines and branches, along with the strange, feathery particles suspended in the thick air that stuck stubbornly to my skin, while Val stayed close at my heels. It was impossible to move fast and be quiet, so I'd given up any pretense of grace and stealth. Now it was all about survival.

We were still running toward the rushing water, and that sound grew louder, which made it harder to hear if the footsteps behind us were closer, or if we'd succeeded in outrunning them. When Val yelped and stumbled to the ground behind me, I stopped.

"Come on," I whispered urgently, grabbing her under the elbow and trying to tug her to her feet.

She winced. "I twisted something."

I cut my gaze to her oddly angled ankle and the vine curled around it, muttering darkly. "You're going to have to push through the pain. Either that or get an arrow through the chest."

She held up a finger and tilted her head. "I don't hear them anymore."

I paused to listen. The trampling footfall behind us had subsided and no more arrows sliced through the air overhead. This didn't mean we were safe, though. Not if this was some sort of sick hunt. It only meant our hunters had taken a break or gotten tired of the chase. They'd be back for us. "We still can't stay here. We need to find a place to hide."

Val nodded, pressing her lips together in obvious pain as she let me pull her to her feet. "I'm going to slow you down, Lia. You should go ahead without me. I'll catch up."

I snorted out a mirthless laugh. "You think I'm going to leave a wounded shipmate to be hunted down by some aliens with a twisted sense of fun? We go together, or we don't go."

"I thought you'd be stubborn about it, but it was worth a try." Val hopped on one foot, her other foot barely touching the ground as I wrapped an arm around her waist. "You're a lot tougher than you look."

I cut her a side eye grin. "I'd have to be, wouldn't I?"

I wasn't particularly tall or muscular, so Val wasn't the first person to be surprised by my tenacity. By now, I was used to overcoming people's low expectations of me.

"Don't get me wrong," the scientist said, as we moved jerkily through the tangled foliage. "No one thinks I look like a scientist."

I glanced at the woman, who was, by any measure, beautiful, with her dark curls and long-lashed, dark eyes. "I guess you don't."

She gave me a mock scowl. "Not all physicists are nerdy guys with glasses."

"Weren't the other members of your team men with receding hairlines and glasses?"

"Aside from Harper and me, maybe they were." Then her expression twisted in pain, and I realized that she was thinking that all those colleagues had been killed by the slavers.

"How did you end up being a scientific researcher for the empire?" I asked to distract her from her grief and to keep my mind off mine.

"Lots of hard work and a little bit of luck." She swept her gaze at the jungle surrounding us. "Not that I feel lucky now."

I pushed some large, blue fronds aside and spit out a puff of pink dust. "We're alive, aren't we?"

"For now." Her voice quavered. "If they really dumped us on the moon where the Xulonians hunt humans for sport, what chance do we have to survive? It's not a fair fight, unless you were given weapons I wasn't. They have arrows, and who knows what else. We have nothing. And it's not like they're going to give up. Even if some of them fail, more will arrive to replace them."

I wasn't sure how the place worked, but that sounded realistic—and horrifying. "I don't know about you, but I refuse to go down without a fight."

She wrinkled her brow at me. "How do we fight? We have nothing to fight *with*."

"Not yet we don't. Remember our plan? Shelter, water, and food, and then we make weapons." I grinned as we stepped from the jungle onto a flat, milky-white rock that extended over a burbling stream. "We've already locked in the water. I'd say we're ahead of schedule on our plan."

Val allowed herself a weak laugh. "I do like being ahead of schedule."

I searched the other bank of the stream for any movement. Emerging from the protection of the jungle meant risking being easy targets, but it would also allow us to hide our trail. I saw no movement behind the blue leaves on the other side of the water, and I let out a hesitant breath. "Are you up for a bit of wading?"

Val eyed the stream that was flowing quickly over glossy, pearlescent stones. "I think I can handle it. The water might be good for my ankle."

I stole a look at her ankle, which was distinctly puffier than it had been when I'd hoisted her from the ground. No doubt that it was sprained, which made our attempts to move fast a lot harder. I needed to cover our tracks and find a place for her to hide until her ankle healed a bit.

"Let's go." I stepped down carefully into the stream, sucking in a quick breath as the icy water swirled around my feet. My boots found purchase on some mud between the rocks, and I helped Val lower herself into the water.

"Son of a Grethneck," she muttered. "At least I won't feel my ankle soon. It'll be completely numb."

I laughed, but she was right. We wouldn't be able to stay in the frigid water for long. I took a step, planting my foot before bringing Val along behind me and leaning forward slightly as the water rushed toward me and pushed my legs back. Soon, we'd developed a rhythm, and we were advancing upstream at a slow but steady pace.

"Should we be worried that it's so quiet?" Val asked after another long stride.

I hated that she'd given voice to my own fears. Before I could reassure her, something bumped into my boot under the water. Glancing down, I saw a silvery-blue eel trying to sink glittering fangs into my boot.

"Duck me!" I brought my other boot down hard on the eel's

head, severing its hold on me. So much for the beautiful, calm stream. The alien eels looked menacing—and carnivorous. I was getting the feeling that the moon was more deadly than it appeared at first glance—hunters or not.

"Duck me?" Val asked, as I scoured the water for more eels.

"I wasn't allowed to curse when I was a kid, but when things got really bad, the nurses would allow some variations on bad words," I explained absently. It had been a long time since one of my childhood curses had slipped out, but when I was really scared, they made me feel better than actual profanity.

Val didn't press me for more details as I dragged her as fast as I could upstream so the eel couldn't return—and bring friends. When I spotted a rock that sloped up from the water and was covered almost entirely in a tangle of vines and brambles, I adjusted our heading toward it.

"Is that...?" Val asked, as we got closer.

I heaved us from the water and onto the rock, pushing aside the prickly branches with one foot to reveal a dark opening. "A cave."

Val sagged against me then tensed. "You don't think anything lives in it, do you?"

I studied the foliage that hung over the mouth. "This hasn't been disturbed for a long time. If a creature lived here, there would be some path or indication that it's been coming and going. It looks deserted."

Val didn't look completely convinced.

"I'll go inside first," I told her, wishing I had some sort of weapon in case I was wrong about the cave being abandoned.

She pulled my arm back as she shook her head. "No, I'm being ridiculous." She put one hand on the rock overhang and bent over as she hopped inside. "I'm sure you're right. Besides, I can't go for much longer without a break."

I held back the hanging vines until she was inside, bending over and peering in. The cave wasn't huge, but it was tall enough for Val to stand with her head almost brushing the ceiling, and it extended far enough back that she could be hidden entirely from view from anyone standing at the mouth. A mound of blue foliage was piled in the back, but otherwise, it was empty.

She held her arms open and smiled at me. "Looks like it's move-in ready."

I mentally checked shelter off my to-do list, even though a little voice in the back of my head didn't like the fact that it was so perfect. Were we being lured into complacency? Was the cave a natural formation, or something designed to attract wounded prey?

I shook off this thought. "Will you be okay here if I go look for food?"

Val's smile faltered but she nodded. "Go. I'll be fine. But be careful, Lia."

"I won't go far. There's bound to be something edible near the water."

"Not eel," she said with a grin.

I returned her smile and dropped the foliage, pleased to see how completely it masked the entrance to the cave.

I turned and scanned the area again, pausing to listen for any movement. When I didn't detect anything but the sound of water bubbling over rocks, I crept along the bank. Now that I wasn't carrying Val, I could move more quietly, my footsteps almost silent as I walked on my toes through the soft dirt. I continued upstream and away from the direction we'd come, my gaze scouring the ground for berries or edible mushrooms.

"I probably should have brought the scientist foraging for food," I said under my breath, making a note not to eat anything I found until I ran it by Val. There was a better chance she'd know the markers of poisonous berries or fungi than I would, although it was an alien moon. Even a trained scientist might not know the poisonous foods of an unknown ecosystem.

A snap behind me made me go still, my heart hammering in my chest, as I braced for the arrow to pierce my flesh. It was too close for me to have any chance of escape by running. When the pain didn't come, I released a breath. It must have been an animal. I almost laughed at my paranoia, but then I heard something thrashing through the jungle in the distance. They'd picked up our trail and were coming for us. My stomach lurched. I had to get back to the cave.

I turned to run but a hand clamped over my mouth and another around my waist, and I was dragged away from the sounds of the pursuers—and away from the scientist in the cave I'd sworn to protect.

NINE

Torst

I heard the arrows before I saw them, the whistling sound distinct as the shiny metal sliced through the air. All thoughts of my mating fever were forgotten as I assumed a battle stance, bending low and flexing my arms as if to brace for an attack. But the attack wasn't aimed at me, and within moments I spotted a pair of dark-haired creatures running through the jungle as more arrows flew over them.

I was so startled to see what I quickly recognized as human females that it took me a moment to shake off my shock and track their escape. What were humans doing on a moon of Xulon? My one encounter with the small, bipedal aliens had been on the Inferno Force ship. The humans were the mates of the Drexians, but I'd been led to believe that their planet, Earth, didn't possess the technology to travel light years through space. It was only because of the Drexians' need for compatible brides that the humans had left their planet at all. And now they were in a faraway galaxy on a distant moon of an alien planet—being hunted.

"The temporal shift," I reminded myself, as I crouched down and made my way through the thick, blue foliage in a parallel path to the fleeing humans. Five hundred astro-years in the future, Earthlings had clearly made it to space without the Drexians, as I didn't see a hint of the valiant warriors with the females.

To their credit, the humans didn't scream as they were pursued. One of the females was helping the other, and their gait was uneven, but they did an admirable job of staying low and using the thick vegetation for cover. Once I saw that they were cleverer than their pursuers, I hung back in an attempt to identify who was chasing them, but either they broke off their hunt or they were well-concealed. By the time I closed in on the origin spot of the arrows, there was nothing but flattened undergrowth.

"Spawn of a Sythian," I muttered when I came upon the empty clearing. Someone had been there, but they'd left.

I decided to go after the females and not the mysterious archer. I needed to know why they were being hunted, and I didn't relish being on the sharp end of an arrow.

Tipping my head back, I drew in a deep breath. The fact that I could detect the humans' scent in the sticky air wasn't something I wished to dwell on, but it would be easier to track them by their scent than by their path. They'd left few broken limbs in their wake, making me believe that one or both had some sort of evasive training. Which made me wonder again, what were they doing here, and what was this place?

I moved on silent feet through the jungle, keeping low and alert in case the hunters returned and mistook me for their prey. My own search for more Taori was pushed aside. Not only did I detect no spires of smoke curling into the sky from downed escape pods, but finding my fellow warriors would not answer my growing curiosity about the moon. The humans might have those answers. At least, they could tell me why they were being pursued.

I refused to admit the other reason why I wanted to find them. Aside from my primal instinct to protect any female in danger, there was another stronger—and more carnal—desire growing within me. The stirrings of my mating fever made my desire to find the females a compulsion I had no power to ignore. My cock twitched, as if also detecting the presence of females as instinctively as my nose, and I pressed a hand to it as it strained against the stiff leather of my low-slung pants.

Grunting with frustration, I made my way stealthily through the jungle until I reached a stream and paused on the bank. I crouched, my fingers sinking into the slick mud, as I spotted tracks of the same mud on the pale stones along the banks. The trail vanished beneath the water, and I smiled at the strategy. The females were traveling up the stream to hide their footprints, but they couldn't mask their scent.

I scooped several handfuls of water into my mouth, grateful for the crisp, clear liquid as it cleansed my throat of the smoke and my mouth of the taste of char. Straightening, I sucked in a breath of the cooler air near the water's edge and picked up their distinctive aroma. Now I understood why Daiken had such a hard time controlling his urges when he'd encountered humans on the Inferno Force ship. Their scent was intoxicating, making my heart hammer erratically and beads of sweat slide down my chest.

"Goddess of the Moon," I said under my breath, "grant me the strength to resist these females."

I walked along the stream, getting ever closer to the

humans. Now, their aroma was almost overpowering, and I could distinguish between the two. One was sweeter than the other, although the variation was subtle. Then I picked up a sharp, bitter smell from behind me. Without looking over my shoulder, my gut told me it was the hunters. I could almost smell their hunger and their brutal desire to kill as if it was rancid and festering within them.

I tightened my grip on the handle of my blade as I dropped to the ground. They were coming toward me but moving too quickly to be noticing details like a Taori lying in wait for them. Breathing in once more, I determined that it was a solo hunter approaching. He'd broken off from the rest, maybe because he was sure he could find the females on his own, or perhaps because he was cleverer than the others and had tracked the humans to the water and deduced their strategy.

It didn't matter. He was hunting the females I knew I must protect, which meant he had to die. I stilled my breathing and my heart rate, focusing my heightened tracking ability on the snaps of twigs and wafts of his odor. When he was almost on top of me, his bow held high with an arrow notched in it as he scanned the overgrown bank of the stream, I rose behind him and circled my arm across his throat, slashing an opening in his neck before he could detect my presence.

For a moment, he remained motionless. Then his bow fell, and his hands clutched his neck, the blood flowing blue between his scarlet fingers. As he twisted slightly, I got a glimpse of his profile—red skin stretched taut across his face and black eyes wide with disbelief. His lipless mouth opened and closed, but the only sound that emerged was a gurgle as more blue blood sputtered from his face and neck. So, this was the alien who'd been hunting the females? I'd never seen a member of the Xulon race, but I assumed this spindly creature was one.

He sank to his knees, and I backed away as he fell forward into a nest of tangled vines, the blue of his blood almost melding with the color of the leaves surrounding him. Aside from his purple, form-fitting outfit that also blended into the jungle, there was no indication why he was on the moon, or why he was tracking the females.

Plucking the shiny, metal bow from the ground, I gave the hunter a final backward glance, as vines started to curl around his lifeless body, before continuing my own pursuit of the humans. I quickly picked up their scent again, but there was no sign of them. I paused behind an outcropping of rocks where the smell of them was so heady it made me knees weak.

"They've been here," I whispered to myself, as I brushed my fingers along the smooth ivory stone. "But where did they go?"

Then I spotted movement along the edge of the water. The female's pants were the color of Vardellen mud, and her shirt was emblazoned with an insignia I didn't recognize. She was slight, compared to me, with skin not as bronze as mine but more like the warm color of the tan rock cliffs of Taor. Glossy, black hair was pulled up high to reveal eyes with an upward sweep at the corners—and she was alone. I followed her without making a sound, creeping closer as her attention was clearly on foraging.

This was the female with the sweeter scent, I realized, as my mouth went dry, and my cock swelled. This was the one who could quench my fever. My fingers tingled in anticipation, and I swallowed a growl. I needed to regain control before I could approach her to talk.

I was so overcome with desire that I forgot to watch my step, and a branch snapped loudly beneath my foot. The female tensed, and I crouched so she wouldn't see me. I was now so close I could have reached out a hand and touched her. Instead, I held my breath.

Before she could spot me, the quiet was shattered by loud sounds of creatures running toward us. The other hunters had found her, and they were coming fast and with reinforcements. There was no time for a calm introduction anymore. I grabbed her from behind, clamping a hand over her mouth as I dragged her with me.

CHAPTER
TEN

Lia

I tried to scream, but the hand covering my mouth was too large and heavy. My terrified sounds were as futile as my struggling.

"Do not fight me, female." The deep voice was a rumble in my ear as the creature dragged me through the jungle with him. My universal translator implant translated almost all alien languages instantly into mine, but cadence and style of language remained. This voice did not sound like the Xulonian from the slaver's ship or a Hettite. But if he wasn't a Xulonian hunter, then who was he?

At least we were moving away from the thrashing sounds coming toward us, and for some reason, I didn't think this alien was one of the ones who'd been shooting at us. If he'd been firing arrows at Val and me, why would he then sneak up and capture me? My pulse quickened. Maybe one of the hunters had decided he wanted to use me for more than just prey. I tried to wiggle from his grip, but he was so much stronger than me that my attempts did nothing but tire me.

Since I was facing away from him, I couldn't see what he looked like, but I could feel how much taller and broader he was than me. His body was like a granite wall I was being held flush to, and his long hair tickled my cheek as he bent over me, his breath feathering across my ear as he inhaled deeply and then exhaled. I shivered from fear, but also something else. Was he smelling me?

"You don't need to fear me, human." His whisper was a deadly purr caressing my skin. "I have no intention of harming you."

Somehow his reassuring words didn't make him seem any less dangerous, but I had no choice but to remain in his hold as he moved us quickly through the jungle. Despite his stealthy speed, the hunters were gaining ground, and I caught a glimpse of something red between the blue and purple tree trunks.

My captor must have seen it as well because he spun me around and deposited me on the ground behind him before swiveling and firing his own bow. There was a yelp, and something hit the ground.

I scooted back on my hands to get a better look at the creature who'd grabbed me. He must have been two or three heads taller than me, although being on the ground could make anyone seem huge. But this guy was enormous—and terrifying. Like I'd suspected, he was solid muscle, with most of it exposed and only covered by black tattoos inking his chest, back, and arms and curling up his neck. Dark hair fell over his shoulders, and a pair of silvery horns curved from above his temples and around his ears. The only garments he wore were a pair of leather pants from which a long, velvety-tipped tail emerged, and heavy boots. I'd seen plenty of aliens as my time working security for the empire, but never one like this.

When he turned, his iridescent-blue eyes pinned me. "Stay down."

I was so startled and entranced by his gaze that I did what he said. I stayed almost flat on my back, as he knelt on his haunches with his gleaming, metal bow at the ready. The sounds of running had slowed, but the aliens hunting me were near, and they were closing in on our location.

I found that I was holding my breath as the massive alien crouched so close to me I could feel the heat radiating off his bare chest. I tried not to stare at the hard swell of his chest muscles and the ridges that made up his stomach, but the markings drew me in. I wanted to trace my fingers along the dark lines and see if his flesh was as hard and unyielding as it looked.

"For duck's sake, Lia," I scolded myself, ripping my gaze from the creature moments before he leapt up and fired an arrow into the air.

There was a scream as his weapon found its mark, and the jungle erupted into chaos. Red figures flew at us, and glittering arrows zipped overhead. I had no time to scream or even to run, and I had no weapon to use to fight back or defend myself. I only had the enormous alien whose tail was swishing as he moved up and down, firing one arrow after another.

When he'd loosed his last arrow, he rushed forward and slammed the steel bow into the crimson skull of one of the hunters running from him. The alien collapsed into a lifeless heap, and the last hunter squeaked as he spun around and ran away. But the tailed creature leapt high through the air and landed on top of him, grasping the alien's head and spinning it swiftly. The crack was decisive, and the dead alien sagged like a puppet with no strings.

Standing and grunting with obvious satisfaction, the heavily inked alien wiped his hands on the front of his pants and pivoted to me. His eyes, though the color of ice, burned molten. His chest heaved from the battle, sweat shimmering on his markings, and his stance was still one of a predator on the hunt.

"Ducking hell," I said, as I scrambled to my feet. Despite him killing the aliens hunting me, I still didn't know why this creature had tracked me and fought off my attackers. If this was the Xulonian hunting moon, then who was to say that he wasn't also a hunter? He'd certainly shown that he could kill.

Instinct and terror drove my shaky legs forward as I ran through the jungle away from him. If I could just get back to the cave where I'd left Val, I could hide and figure out our next move —and try to determine who on the moon was friend or foe. Even though the tailed creature had just saved my life, something about the way he looked at me told me he might be just as dangerous to me as the hunters.

My heart pounded so hard—the blood a rushing torrent in my ears—that I didn't hear him pursuing me until he'd tackled me to the ground. The air left my body in a whoosh, and I could only gape up at him wordlessly when he flipped me over and trapped me beneath him, his hard body pressed against mine and my hands pinned over my head.

His gaze burned hot as he leaned down and spoke into my ear, his dark stubble rasping my cheek. "I warned you not to fight me, female."

CHAPTER
ELEVEN

Torst

My body trembled as I hovered above her, one hand holding her thin wrists together over her head and my other elbow braced on the ground so I wouldn't crush her. Now that I had the chance to look at her closely, I saw just how much smaller she was than me. But even though she was no match for my bulk, she continued to strain against me.

I bent my head so I could breathe in more of her scent, although I knew I shouldn't tempt myself. "I warned you not to fight me, female."

She released a weary sigh. "What do you want with me, if you aren't going to kill me?"

I reared back. "Why would I kill you?" I registered the fear in her eyes, and the realization hit me that it was me she was afraid of now, not the hunters. I released her wrists and sat back, although I remained straddling her waist so she wouldn't try to run and force me to chase her again. "Why were all those aliens so intent on killing you? What crime have you committed?

Rubbing her wrists, she met my gaze with a quizzical one of her own. "My only crime is being a human and running into Hettite slavers."

I tilted my head at her. I didn't know any aliens called Hettites, but the word slaver made my tail twitch. "You're a slave?"

She scowled at this. "I'm nobody's property." She cut her gaze to where my knees were boxing in her hips. "Now, would you mind getting off me?"

I eyed her. "Do you give me your word not to run from me?"

"That depends. Do you promise you aren't one of the hunters?"

Now I frowned as I rolled off her into a crouch. "The Taori do not hunt human females."

"Taori." She repeated the word as she studied my face. "Is that what you are?"

I grunted my version of a yes. "I am a member of the sky clan of the Taori, a warrior in the Immortal Army. One of the valiant Ten Thousand."

"That's a mouthful," she said under her breath. "And this Immortal Army isn't part of the hunt?"

This human wasn't making any sense. "I have said before, the Taori do not hunt weaker species."

"Who are you calling weak?"

"You have courage," I told her, not adding that she was also foolish and overconfident, "but humans are no match for the Taori."

She shot me a dark look. "If I had a blaster, you wouldn't be saying that."

"If you had a blaster, I would quickly disarm you."

Her eyes widened, and the corner of her mouth twitched. "Cocky much?"

I didn't understand what my cock had to do with anything, although I was glad that my thrumming desire for her had faded, and my cock no longer ached for release.

"Listen, I appreciate the save and all, but why are you here, if you aren't one of the hunters?" Then she put a hand to her mouth. "Are you being hunted, too?"

I shook my head, confused by her questions. "My escape pod crashed on this moon after the planet of Xulon destroyed our ship."

"So, you don't know?" When I gave her a severe look, she held up her hands. "Sorry, but I had no idea you weren't a part of this. Talk about bad luck."

I was quickly losing patience with this human. "Part of what?"

"I hate to be the one to break it to you, big guy, but you crash landed on one of the Xulonian recreation moons."

"Recreation moons?" My universal translator had no problem deciphering the words, but they made no sense together.

"They call them Moorla moons." She stood and wiped her palms on her pants. "I'd never heard of them, either. I guess Xulon likes to keep it quiet that they buy aliens from slavers and use them to entertain their wealthy citizens."

I glanced at the jungle around us. "This is a pleasure planet?"

She wrinkled her nose. "You wish. From what they told us, there is one moon called the lust moon, but the Xulonians only like to watch. Since they apparently dump violently horny aliens on it along with human women, it doesn't sound like pleasure is the point."

A rumble shook my chest at the thought of females being claimed against their will, and my lip curled up in disgust.

"From what I can tell, we're not on that one," the female continued. "The rest of the moons are either set up as hunts or games or whatever else the Xulonians consider recreational."

I swiveled my head, and my gaze caught on the inert body of one of the hunters sprawled on the ground. "This is certainly the hunting moon."

"That's what I thought. Talk about crap luck for both of us, right?" She reached behind her and tugged her tail of hair tighter. "Not that I would have wanted to be on the lust planet being chased by horny aliens."

"No? You would choose death over mating?"

Her mouth gaped, and her gaze dropped. "I'm guessing what the Xulonians like to watch isn't as simple as mating. You have to be pretty serious pervs to set up entire moons for slaughtering other species, or to watch them get it on."

She would get no argument from me. I was still seething over watching the Taori ship being blown to bits. "After I get us off this moon, I will make the Xulonians pay for their crimes."

She stared at me. "How do you plan to leave? It sounds like your escape pod was a one-way trip."

I wasn't sure, but I knew that my fate did not end here. "This is not the end of my story. Nor is it the end of yours. There must be other Taori who landed here. Once I regroup with my fellow warriors, we will devise a plan of escape and revenge."

"I'd like to get some revenge. These assholes are responsible for the rest of my shipmates being slaughtered or dumped on the other moons." Her jaw clenched. "I have friends out there I'd like to see again."

"We will find your friends."

She put her hands on her hips and scrunched her lips to one side. "Why are you so hell-bent on helping me?" She held up a finger. "And if you say it's because I'm weaker than you, I'll show you just how weak a knee to your balls feels."

A laugh welled up in my chest. I liked that this female did not shrink from challenging me. "I can see that you have a courageous spirit. Let us just say that the Taori despise species who victimize others. Since we are both victims of these Xulonians, we should help each other." I didn't tell her that I was pulled to her as if she was the cool shade, and I'd been battling under the scorching sun. Or that my mating fever had heightened my sense of smell, and her scent was as intoxicating as Grillian ale. "Our meeting was written in the stars."

She eyed me. "You're a smooth talker for a big brute of a guy, but I guess teaming up makes sense." She darted a glance around us. "I'm sure those aren't the last hunters we'll see. I have a feeling they hunt until they make their kill."

The tremble in her chin made fury flame fresh within my core followed quickly by a hot burst of longing. I forced myself to ignore the desire as I bowed my head to her. "I am Torst, security chief for Kalesh Naz, and you have my word that I will kill anyone who tries to hurt you."

She gave a shaky laugh. "I believe you, Torst. I'm Lia, a member of the imperial security detail for transport ship 867."

"Lia," I repeated, savoring her name as a thrill went through me. "Our fates are now bound together like twin stars."

"I'm not here alone, so you're going to have to make that triplet stars." Lia beckoned for me to follow her. "I'll take you to meet Valeria—she goes by Val—and our hiding spot."

I fell in step behind her, my eyes sweeping the calm jungle for any danger, as a dark voice in the back of my brain reminded me that the feverish desire I'd felt when I'd touched her was by far her biggest threat.

TWELVE

The Xulonian praetor leaned his bony hands on the levitating desktop, the crimson skin taut over the sharp knuckles. He rapped his pointy nails on the surface as he studied the report. "The alien ship is destroyed?"

The ensign nodded, his bulbous eyes never leaving the floor. "Its weaponry was no match for our phasic missiles."

"Have we identified the ship and which species dared encroach on Xulon territory?"

"Negative. The energy signature and the design of the ship are unknown to us."

The praetor snapped his head up, and the cloak fell from his face. "Unknown? How is that possible? We know every alien species in the galaxy—and they know to steer clear of our sovereign space."

The ensign shifted from one thin, bowed leg to the next. "Our sensors recorded an energy fluctuation before their arrival."

"Did they dare use jump technology to surprise us?"

"The energy patterns were not consistent with jump technology."

The praetor curled his hands into knobby fists. "Is this a new enemy attempting to meddle in our affairs?" Then he shook his head as if dismissing the thought. "No matter, they have been dealt with, as are all those who dare challenge Xulon."

The younger Xulonian darted a glance at his superior. "There is a chance that not all those aboard the alien ship were killed."

"What?" The praetor stilled, narrowing his insect-like eyes until they were slits. "How is that possible?"

"In the final attack, the enemy released a great deal of laser fire. It was useless against us, but it did appear to provide cover for multiple escape pods."

A hiss of breath was released between lips so thin they almost appeared nonexistent. "Escape pods should not be difficult to track and destroy. Their propulsion cannot be significant, if their battleship's technology is any indicator."

"The pods did not attempt to escape our sector, Praetor. From what we can tell, they have landed on our moons."

The praetor stilled. "There are alien escapees on our Moorla moons?"

"It's unknown how many, or if they all survived, but the tactical director of the hunt moon has reported unusual activity."

"Unusual how?"

The ensign cleared his throat. "Multiple dimensional incarnations were terminated during their pursuit of the new human recruits."

The praetor jerked as if startled. "Were the bodies gathered for repair?"

"The incarnations are being restored as we speak, Praetor. They will be ready to be inhabited very soon."

The elder Xulonian pursed his lips. "This happened while

hunting females? How is that possible? They were unarmed and physically weak."

"Either they are not as weak as you suspected." The younger Xulonian dropped his gaze again. "Or the kills were made by one of the aliens from the escape pods."

"What about the footage of the hunt? There must be some recording from the implanted cameras within the dimensional incarnations."

"That is being retrieved, Praetor, but early footage shows only glimpses of a mysterious attacker. No species known to us."

An impatient breath was huffed. "And what of the esteemed citizens who were inhabiting the dimensionals?"

"They were taken by surprise, but all the participants know the risks of venturing onto the hunt moon. It isn't like the others. They know there is a slim chance of being defeated."

The praetor slammed a palm onto his desktop and the hovering surface wobbled. "But they do not expect to lose at the hands of frail humans. The hunt is still stacked in the hunters' favor—for a reason. Unhappy citizens who do not win the hunt do not wish to return."

"There are other moons they can enjoy. The lust moon is flush with new humans." The ensign's words died on his lips, his red skin now shiny with perspiration as he saw the older alien's severe expression. "Of course, this is unacceptable and cannot happen again. Do you wish us to suspend the hunt until we determine who is killing our incarnations?"

"Suspend the hunt? Think of all the revenue that would be lost." The praetor straightened and clasped his hands behind his back. "No, the hunt will continue, but it will do so with promises to our citizens who were terminated that they will have a chance to continue their hunt." He flapped a hand distractedly. "Or they can enjoy a luxury viewing box on the lust moon, if they've lost their taste for blood and prefer to see a female plowed by an insatiable Keera."

"Yes, Praetor." The ensign started to back from the room.

"One last thing," the elder Xulonian said. "Send a complement or two of mercenaries to take out the unwanted aliens." A cool smile stretched his lipless mouth. "Let's see how these mystery creatures do against true hunters."

CHAPTER
THIRTEEN

Lia

I threaded my way through the jungle as the light filtering through the canopy of leaves grew dimmer, and I brushed away a cloud of floating pink dust motes as I glanced back at Torst. "Not much farther."

He grunted in response, a sound I was getting used to from him. I turned back around quickly, ignoring the moisture on my palms.

It's the air, I told myself as I carefully stepped around fallen tree trunks and vines winding across the loamy soil, kicking off purple tendrils that curled toward my feet. The air on the jungle moon *was* thick and humid. My damp palms weren't because of the huge, bare-chested Taori walking behind me. They couldn't be.

I needed to keep my mind focused on surviving and getting Val off the moon safely. I might not be on the imperial transport anymore, but I still had a job to do and a responsibility to the people we'd been ferrying. I couldn't be distracted by a decidedly dangerous alien who made my heart stutter in my chest.

I flashed back to lying underneath him with my arms pinned over my head, and I gave an involuntary shake of my head. I shouldn't have liked any part of that, since I despised feeling weak and powerless, but being trapped beneath him with his hard body pressed to mine had made me want to moan out loud.

"Thank the stars I didn't do that," I muttered, sweeping aside a grouping of hanging vines and a floating, transparent creature with dangling tentacles that swayed in my direction.

"What?"

I cut a quick look over my shoulder. "Nothing. Almost there."

He let out a guttural sound that was one of the rough, throaty noises that seemed to mean any number of things, but even that low rumble sent an unwanted tingle of desire down my spine.

Get it together, Lia, I told myself. It had been so long since I'd felt anything for a guy that the mixture of excitement and nerves was unfamiliar. All I knew was that it wasn't the time for a crush or a fling or anything. I needed to be in survival mode, not thinking about how solid his inked muscles were or wondering if the massive hardness pressing against my stomach had been his...

I jumped when his hand closed around my arm and pulled me to a stop. He held a finger to his mouth, and we both stilled and listened. Since Torst had killed the red-skinned hunters, the jungle had been almost peacefully quiet. Either that had been the extent of the hunting party, or the rest of the hunters were busy someplace else.

I couldn't get a good sense of how large the moon was, and if it was all jungle, or if this was only one of many environments covering the surface. Our surroundings seemed organic, but was it possible we were in a holographic simulation? I frowned as I dismissed that thought. If this was a simulation, whomever was controlling it would have stopped it once their hunters were massacred. Besides, if it was a simulation, there would be no need for physical moons, and the Xulonian and the Hettite slaver had both talked about the moons as real places. Not to mention, the alien following me had crashed here in an escape pod. Unfortunately, that meant that all of this was real.

Swatting at an encroaching vine, I glanced at Torst, whose attention was focused on the milky, pink sky as he held me still. Even his tail, which usually twitched behind him, was unmoving as it hovered in an upward arch behind him. Just as I was about to ask him what we were looking at, a ship skimmed the treetops above us.

It was low enough that I could see the shiny, white hull and the vessel's snub nose. I wasn't an expert on aircraft, but it looked like a transport and not a fighter or a security patrol.

"They're bringing more of their kind to the surface," Torst said, his grip on my arm not relaxing.

"It could be a shipment of more of us." I didn't think this was true, but I'd rather think of more targets arriving than more hunters.

He shook his head, and his long hair swung slightly around his shoulders. "They know about the dead hunters. These are either replacements—or something worse."

"Something worse?" My gut clenched. "What's worse than hunters with weapons when you don't have any?"

Torst held my gaze for a beat then huffed out a rough sound. "Many things."

Fear iced my skin, and I rubbed the prickly bumps on my exposed flesh briskly. I hated to admit that I was scared, and I hated even more having to acknowledge that I might be in over my head. Torst had already saved me from being killed, and if more hunters—or something worse—were coming for us, I feared I wouldn't be a match for them.

I pressed my lips together until they hurt. This is just your mother and the other cadets talking, I told myself. My mother's voice I could push aside, but the jeers of the bigger and stronger males I'd trained with echoed in my head no matter how much I tried to ignore them. It didn't matter that I'd been the top marksman in our class, or that my aptitude for military strategy bested every one of them. I had been smaller and less powerful, which had meant that I got slammed to the ground in almost every grappling match. I'd gotten used to the bruises, but the doubt had never left me.

"Lia?"

Torst's low rumble of a voice pulled me back to reality. I honed in on his face—his intensely blue eyes and his brow furrowed in concern. "If there are more hunters coming for us, I need to get back to Val. She's been alone for too long, and I promised her I'd be right back."

He dropped my arm, and I picked up the pace, swatting away branches as I made my way toward the water and the hidden cave. For a terrifying moment, I feared that I'd overshot it, or that I'd lost it entirely. My heart tripped in my chest, as I thought of Val hiding in the dark, injured and waiting.

Then I centered myself and took a deep breath, scanning the vegetation and rocks lining the stream and finally locking in on familiar markers.

"This is it," I said, not caring that I let out a loud sigh of relief as I strode up to the heavily covered cave opening.

Torst gave what I took to be an approving nod. "It is almost impossible to discern that it isn't part of the jungle."

I grinned at him. "It wasn't easy to find shelter, but it should be a good place to hide from any new hunters."

A flicker of something passed over the Taori's face, but it was gone in an instant, and he motioned with his head for me to go inside.

I bent slightly and pushed aside the thick curtain of vines, the interior of the stone enclosure bathed in darkness. "Val, I'm back, and I found someone who can help us."

Torst followed me inside, crouching to fit. Even without him touching me, his body seemed to fill the smaller space. I shuffled farther inside as my eyes adjusted to the dark, and I searched the back of the cave for the scientist I'd left.

"Val?" My voice echoed back to me, but there was no response. Even without much light, I could see that she wasn't there. I turned to Torst, and my voice cracked when I spoke. "I left her right here."

"Maybe she ventured out for food or water."

I shook my head, as I tried to control the panic rising within me. "She wouldn't have left. She was injured. Her ankle couldn't support her weight."

Torst got on all fours and moved along the rock floor. "There is no blood or signs that she was taken violently."

That was small comfort when I knew that Val couldn't have left the cave by herself. I squeezed my hands into fists so tight my knuckles hurt. I'd failed in my mission, and I'd failed her.

CHAPTER
FOURTEEN

Torst

Lia's shoulders slumped for a moment, but then she squared them and stood as straight as she could in the cave. "I'm going to find her."

I grabbed her arm as she headed for the opening. "I share in the pain for your fallen, but sacrificing yourself will not bring her back."

"Yes, it will, because I'm going to literally go get her back. She isn't fallen. She's out there somewhere, and the sooner we go looking, the better."

"You cannot."

Tipping her head up to meet my gaze, her own eyes blazed with anger. "What do you mean I can't? I just met you, smooth talker. I appreciate the save and all, but you can't tell me what I can and can't do."

"The jungle is losing light. You can't wander in the dark

looking for your wounded friend. You have no way to see, and no weapon."

Her glare hardened. "You're welcome to come with me, but I'm going." Her voice broke on the last word. "Val is out there somewhere, and it's my job to keep her safe."

I let out an exasperated breath. I knew little of humans, but were they all so impossible? "You must hear the whisper of death like a familiar companion."

"I don't know what that means." She jutted out one hip. "But it doesn't sound like a compliment."

"It means you seem to enjoy courting danger like it is a seductive lover." I watched her mouth drop. "I will go search for this Val. You will stay here."

She regained her composure and cleared her throat. "Are you ordering me around? Just because..." she waved a hand at me "...you're big and brawny doesn't mean you can give me orders. I don't serve under you and—"

"If you served on a Taori ship, you'd have already landed in the brig."

She barked out a laugh. "For what, not obeying you?"

I stepped closer. "For insubordination that risks the mission." I dearly wished I had access to a brig into which I could throw her. Then my thoughts drifted to how much I'd enjoy seeing her in restraints, and heat pooled restlessly in my core. Gods of the ancients, it took all my control not to crush my mouth to hers to quiet her protests.

Her eyes widened. "Insubordination? You're assuming that you'd be my superior."

"I serve as the chief of security on a Taori battleship. You told me you are a security officer on a transport ship. I outrank you, female."

"In case you haven't noticed, we aren't on our ships anymore, so rank doesn't matter." She jabbed a finger at my chest. "And if you think I'm going to step in line just because you're bigger and stronger and a male, then you're crazy."

I growled, and the rumble filled the compact cave. Why was this female insisting on fighting me? Didn't she see that I only wanted to protect her? My skin sizzled with heat as I stood so close to her I could feel her warm breath on my chest. As much as I battled my urge to claim her, I could not suppress my Taori duty to keep her safe. Not when my body ached to hold her and shield her from danger.

"And all that growling and grunting doesn't intimidate me," she added, although she took a small step back.

"I am not trying to intimidate you, female." I gritted out the words. "I'm trying to protect you from aliens who wish you dead."

"I can take care of myself."

I raised an eyebrow, and even in the low lighting, I detected her pupils flaring.

"Usually, I can take care of myself," she corrected. "When I'm not dumped on an alien moon with no weapons. Besides, it isn't your responsibility to take care of me. You don't even know me."

This was true, but I had a strange sensation of familiarity around the female. Whether it was the mating fever or something deeper, I felt like I did know her. I might have only laid eyes on her a short while ago, but I already knew without a shred of doubt that it was my duty to keep her alive—at whatever cost to myself.

A curious certainly overcame me. I would willingly sacrifice my own life for this human's. I grunted again, not pleased with this realization and cursing it in my head.

"As I told you before, female, our fates are now interwoven. I cannot untangle your future from mine."

She stared at me, and I wondered if her universal translator had malfunctioned. "What are you talking about? We just met."

"I am Taori, one of the Immortals who ride into the valley of death. We do not send females into danger." I didn't mention how deep my devotion to her went. If she thought I was crazy before, that would not help change her mind.

She shook her head as if dislodging something from her ear. "You're not sending me anywhere. I'm going."

"Can you see through the veil of darkness?" I asked, my sharp words cutting off her reply.

She blinked at me. It was dim inside the cave, and I could see she was squinting.

"Of course, I can't see in the dark." She shook her head as if I was asking foolish questions, then she stopped and held my gaze. "Wait, can you?"

"The Taori's eyes adjust in lower lighting; so, yes, we have visual acuity in the dark—figures appears to us as shades of gray so we can detect movement."

She opened her mouth and then closed it again as if my statement had rendered her speechless.

"I will go look for your friend." I didn't add that my impending mating fever was granting me an even more highly attuned sense of smell. I probably wouldn't need to use my eyes at all. I could scent the female. I'd picked up her smell earlier when I'd tracked them both, and I could do it again.

"But you don't know what she looks like."

"I will find all the injured females and bring them back to you." I did not have time to argue with the female. Ships were already descending with reinforcement hunters—or perhaps an even more menacing predator. I couldn't waste any more time debating her, but I also could not take her with me. She would only slow my pursuit. "You can stay here of your own free will, or I can tie you up."

She sucked in a breath. "You wouldn't."

I curled a hand around the back of her neck, tipping her face up and locking my gaze on hers. My eyes drifted to her lips, and desire hummed down the length of my spine and tail, until the tip quivered. "To save your friend and keep you safe, I would bind and gag you, and enjoy every moment of it."

"You might use pretty words but you're still a brute," she whispered. "Maybe you're no better than the ones who were hunting me."

I didn't tell her that once the mating fever consumed me, I would be every bit as dangerous to her. "Do you truly believe that, Lia?"

Her shallow breaths tickled my throat as she shook her head. "No."

Her voice was tinged with fear. I didn't want her to be afraid of me, but I could live with her fear if it meant she didn't end up dead. "I will find your friend. I promise. But you must promise me that you won't follow me. I can hunt faster alone."

Her pupils flared at the word hunt, but she nodded. Before I could determine if I believed her or if I should bind her with vines, a sound outside the cave reached my ears. It wasn't close, but it also wasn't the rustle of an animal moving through the undergrowth. It was the measured footfall of a hunting party.

I closed my hand over Lia's mouth and dragged her to the back of the cave, whispering into her ear so softly the words were almost silent. "The new hunters have found us."

FIFTEEN

Torst

As soon as I whispered the warning into her ear, Lia stopped struggling. I used the bulk of my body as a barrier between her and the opening of the cave, curling myself over her and tucking her head beneath mine.

The sound of feet crunching on leaves remained steady, and I allowed myself a slow breath as I listened for any sudden shift in their direction. If they were tracking us from where we'd left the bodies of the hunters, they would soon be upon us. I cursed myself for not insisting we double back or tramp through the stream.

I'd been too distracted by the female and by my overwhelming desire for her, the flickering hints of the approaching fever creating chaos within my body and mind. But it was impossible not to be overwhelmed with carnal hunger when every breath was filled with her scent.

I clenched my teeth and vowed to be stronger than the

fever. I could not allow it to render me so mad with lust that I didn't protect the female I'd vowed to save. I was Taori, I reasoned. I was bred and trained to be fierce and unfailing. I would not fail in this.

"How many of these aliens are we hunting?"

The voice sounded like it was coming from right outside the mouth of the cave. Lia stiffened beneath me but didn't make a sound. My heart thundered so loudly I hoped none of the new hunters had powerful hearing. An apex predator would have easily heard me.

"We don't know that, do we?" another voice snapped. "All that praetor told us was that they think at least two pods from the ship they blew up made it down here. Maybe more."

I couldn't place the alien accents, but I was in a galaxy far from mine, and I was hundreds of astro-years from my time. I only knew they were male, and they emitted no tell-tale scent of fear. That meant they were either well-trained and confident in their hunting skills or so well-armed that there was no doubt any prey could survive their onslaught.

"We only found the one pod. He's sure there are more?"

"Didn't you hear me? I said he *thinks* there were two. They were too busy firing on the big ship to track those pods."

A snort of derision. "Don't know why anyone thought it would be a good idea to escape to here."

"Maybe they don't know where here is. It sounded like the ship wasn't anything Xulon had seen before."

"I don't like it," a third, higher voice said. "A ship appears from nowhere in Xulon space and then it sends a bunch of pods to the surface of their moons? What if it's someone who knows about all this?"

"How could anyone know? Xulon doesn't allow anyone to come near their territory. They don't have diplomatic relations with other planets. The only other species they deal with are the slavers and us."

"And that's just because they know we don't care what they do as long as they pay well."

A rough laugh. "They sure do pay well."

"And they're paying extra for us to take out whatever landed on the moon that isn't supposed to be here."

Mercenaries, I thought as revulsion swirled in my gut. I despised soldiers of fortune who didn't possess honor or purpose. They were the antithesis of everything the Taori stood for. I didn't care if they were only hired hands in this sick hunt. They were as guilty as the ones who hired them, and I looked forward to killing them one by one.

Lia jerked her head up, and I realized that I'd made a sound. I slid a hand to the blade on my waistband, preparing to return an attack and defend Lia.

"You don't think it's some sort of beast?" the higher voice asked.

"A beast?" Another mercenary choked on a laugh. "What kind of beast can launch an escape pod?"

"Maybe the aliens in the ship sent beasts down as some kind of payback."

The rest of the group laughed, and I released a relieved yet silent breath. They hadn't heard me, and they had no idea they were standing outside a cave in which one of their targets was hiding.

"Enough of this talk of beasts. We got ourselves a few aliens running around. That's all."

"Aliens who killed all the Xulonians in the hunt."

"The dimensional incarnations," another corrected. "The Xulonians are too scared to leave their planet, even to come to one of their own moons."

I wasn't sure what this meant, but I liked the sound of the Xulonians less and less.

"How weak do you have to be if you're scared to go on a real hunt, even when your prey is unarmed?"

"None of those scrawny, red-skulls could ever catch anything if the odds were even."

"It's not like they have things to hunt on their home world. Any big game died off long ago cause of all that mining. Where would they learn?"

"It's still not a real hunt if they're chasing down unarmed humans. Where's the thrill in that?"

"Well, whatever killed the hunters wasn't a puny human."

More low muttering. "If it was ferocious enough to do all that damage, where did it go? Where's it hiding?"

"We know it left that burned-out escape pod and took out the hunting party. After that, it must have been hungry and thirsty. I say we keep going down the river. Chances are it's camped out near the water."

"I sure wish we'd been sent on assignment to the lust moon," one of the mercenaries said with a gurgling laugh. "I'd rather watch females get chased and fucked than be stuck hunting down some renegade alien."

"Well, that's not our job, and you know only their citizens get to watch."

"It's not normal, if you ask me. Who'd want to watch if you could be the one fucking them?"

"The red-skulls aren't normal. Don't you get that by now? They pay good, but living on a dead planet has made them twisted."

"Least they pay good. Not that we're gonna get paid if we don't kill this alien."

"And the other alien—if there is one?"

"The other team can track that one. We got our hands full,

and we got to take out this alien before the next hunt begins. There's a bonus in it for us."

The voices moved away as the mercenaries started talking about what each would do with their share of the payment. When I heard distant splashing, I allowed myself to relax and grin.

There was a good chance there was another Taori on the moon with me. My spirits lifted at the thought of finding one of my kinsmen. Any escape plan would be easier with another warrior by my side, especially now that I had Lia to protect and her friend to locate. I also knew the rough number of mercenaries hunting for us—and that they weren't very bright or very quiet. They would be easy to track and kill.

"They're gone," Lia said softly. "You can get off me now."

I'd almost forgotten I was shielding her body with my own. The feel of her smaller body tucked into mine felt natural, as if she belonged there.

I stepped back, already missing the heat of her as the dank cave air hit my chest. But before I could move away completely, she let out a breathy sigh. The sound went straight to my cock, which pulsed with an urgency that nearly made my knees buckle.

My vision blurred as my ears were filled with the deafening rush of blood, and her sweet scent seemed to envelope me. Fire throbbed through my veins, and I twisted my head to one side in an attempt to control my urge to pin her against the wall and bury my cock between her legs. Even though I was powerless to stop it, I knew the fever was advancing far quicker than it ever had before.

Of course, I'd never had to fight it off before. In the past, when the Quaibyn had come, as it did every ten astro-years or so, I'd been prepared. I'd quenched my hunger with one of the Quaibyn priestesses on Taor or one of the pleasure planets scattered throughout the galaxies. But now, there would be no easy relief.

Instead of grabbing Lia like I wished, I braced a hand on the cave wall, the cool stone grounding me as I attempted to quell my driving need. I squeezed my eyes shut and held my breath, hoping that if I couldn't inhale her aroma, I might be able to restrain myself. But even without drawing in breath, I could detect the scent of her...arousal?

My eyes flew open. Lia's own dark eyes held mine and her hands were pressed against my chest. In my feverish state, I didn't know if she was pushing me away or longing for my touch. In the grip of the Quaibyn, I knew nothing.

Wrenching myself away from her, I staggered toward the opening of the cave, bursting out through the tangle of vines, not caring if I met with a band of bloodthirsty mercenaries. Anything to burn off my lust and keep me from claiming Lia whether she wanted me or not.

CHAPTER
SIXTEEN

Lia

I pressed a hand to my heart, the hammering in my chest reverberating through my fingers. What had just happened? My eyes had adjusted enough to the darkness that I could see the iridescent blue of Torst's eyes, but when he'd looked down at me just then they hadn't been their usual color. The blue had been the thinnest of circles around the black pupil, yet they'd burned with an internal fire—and something dark and animalistic.

Swallowing hard, I eyed the opening of the cave. He'd staggered out without touching me, but his torment had been palpable. I'd sensed desire in him before, and my own arousal had been ignited when he'd pinned me to the ground earlier, but this was something wilder and more uncontrolled. For the first time since he'd saved my life, I longed for a weapon to protect me from the Taori.

"Come on, Lia," I thought, in a weak attempt to convince myself that I was overreacting. "It wasn't all that."

Maybe I had been imagining things. It wasn't like I'd never been hit on before, or even groped a few times at some of the rougher outposts. And Torst hadn't actually groped me. Sure, he'd pinned me down and threatened to tie me up, but that was more about getting me to do what he said than getting me to drop my pants. At least, that's what I had to believe. Otherwise, I was stranded on an alien moon being tracked by mercenaries, and my only ally was having a hard time keeping from tearing off my clothes. Not a comforting thought.

I slid down the rock wall until I was sitting with my knees bent, and I wrapped my arms around them. Whatever was going on with Torst—or whatever I was imagining—the fact remained that Val was missing, and we were both still being hunted. Only now, Torst was also a target.

I let my head droop until my forehead touched my knees. "This is not going well."

What did you expect?

My mother's voice was so clear in my mind I snapped my head up, half expecting her to be standing in front of me.

I blew out a breath when I realized how ridiculous that was. My mother was back on our home world. "Don't be foolish, Lia."

Guilt gnawed at my relief that my mother wasn't reprimanding me in person. I hadn't seen her since I joined the imperial military academy, and she'd told me I'd never make it through. Her words had been a betrayal I couldn't forgive, even though they'd also driven me to work harder than I ever had in my life.

It hadn't mattered to me that she'd had good reason to worry, or that she was probably terrified that the daughter who'd spent most of her childhood sick and in medical wards wouldn't survive in such a physically demanding career. That was exactly why I'd needed to do it. After feeling frail and powerless for so long, I needed to prove to myself and the universe that I could survive anything.

"So much for that," I whispered to myself, hearing the quaver in my voice, and hating the weakness that still slipped through in my darkest moments.

My plan to be so tough that nothing could hurt me had landed me in the middle of a situation I probably wasn't going to survive. A part of me ached that I'd never see my mother again, even though another part of me—the stubborn part that had always gotten me into trouble—still nursed the painful wound of her not believing in me. Even so, I hoped she'd never learn of my fate and how I'd squandered the life she and my father had fought so hard for me to have.

My eyes stung with tears I refused to shed. It was more weakness I couldn't afford. Not when I needed to figure out a plan to find Val. I wasn't sure how much I could rely on the Taori. As huge and deadly as he was, he had his own shipmates to find, and there was no denying that Val and I would not be an asset to his survival.

As if he sensed I was thinking about him, Torst stepped back inside the cave, the foliage rustling as it fell back into place behind him. The only light came from a faint glow of what I assumed was moonlight, but my eyes had adjusted to the darkness. If what he'd said about his vision was true, he could see me clearly.

I straightened, my body naturally on high alert. Even in the shadowy dimness, his eyes shone blue again, a brightness than was almost a glow.

"I owe you an apology," he said, "and an explanation."

His demeanor had changed entirely, and instead of pulsing

with need and practically vibrating with the desire to pounce, the Taori was calm, drained even.

"You didn't do anything to me, aside from startle me a bit." I managed a weak smile. The last thing I wanted was to be seen as some kind of fragile flower who swooned if a male looked at her funny. I'd been around enough inebriated men at grimy outpost cantinas to know how to defend myself, although if I was being honest, Torst would have had no problem overpowering me. But he hadn't, so I wasn't going to hold a grudge because he'd gotten hot and bothered. Okay, very hot and extremely bothered.

"Not tonight, but I can't promise I'll be able to hold myself back forever." He lowered himself slowly to the floor, sitting across from me, but close enough that I could make out his glittering eyes, the dark scruff on his cheeks, and the silvery, curved horns on his head.

"O-kay." How did a girl respond to a guy telling her he might force himself on her in the future? If this was the way the Taori charmed women, I didn't get it.

Torst's closed his eyes for a beat. "Please know that I would never knowingly harm you, but once the fever takes over, I will no longer be in control. If I didn't think you would be killed by the hunters and now the mercenaries, I would beg you to run as far from me as possible."

My throat tightened. "You're sick?"

"The fever is more a curse than an illness, but it isn't something that I can cure or hope will pass." He bowed his head. "Once it overtakes me, there is only one way to burn off the heat."

I waited for him to tell me how he could be cured, but he was silent. I shifted, crossed my legs, and leaned forward. I understood the strong and silent type, and I could even handle the strange way he worded things, but there was being mysterious and then there was being deliberately confusing. "You want to tell me the one way you can get rid of this fever or do you—"

"The only way to burn off my quickly advancing Taori mating fever is for me to fuck a compatible female," he said so abruptly that I jerked back.

My face burned at his abrupt words, but I shook off the embarrassment. I'd gone through the imperial military academy and served on more than a few security teams with males who were cruder than that. If he thought I'd be scared off by his language, he was wrong. Then I digested what he'd said. "Mating fever? That's a real thing?"

He met my gaze and one of his eyebrows quirked. "You believe I would weave this affliction from the air?"

I twitched a shoulder. "I've heard worse lines."

His nose wrinkled. "Lines?"

"You know, something you tell a female to get her on her back."

"I did not need a line to get you on your back. You are quite small."

I rolled my eyes. "It's a figure of speech, meaning how can I be sure you aren't telling me this, so I'll... do you?"

Now he jerked in response to my words, his mouth falling open. "No honorable Taori would spin a lie to entice a mate." Then he pulled himself up abruptly. "We do not need deception to get females to our furs."

I could believe that. By any measure, he was breathtaking, with enough brawn and bad-boy energy to make most women go weak at the knees. I decided to believe that he wasn't making up mating fever as a seduction ploy. Besides, I'd seen his wild eyes and felt the heat radiating from him. That hadn't been a trick.

I held up my palms when I saw how much I'd offended him.

"I believe you. I've just never encountered an alien with mating fever. I've heard of it in some species, but none that I've personally met. It sounds like something that's made up."

He grunted roughly. "I would not fabricate this torment."

Torst appeared so wretched as his shoulders hunched forward that I reached out and touched his knee. "If this is something that happens to your people regularly, there must be ways to deal with it."

He lifted his head and met my gaze pointedly.

My cheeks warmed again. "Aside from..."

"Taori males have been cursed with this fever for millennia, but it only occurs once approximately every ten astro-years, so it has been something we've managed. With a Taori's true mate, the fever can be sated after one mating clench, but it can also take many settings of the sun. On our home world, unmated males can engage a female priestess at one of the many Quaibyn houses. Even those of us who chose to leave Taor on a journey we knew would have no return, planned for the fever, although we did not expect it now."

"What do you mean?"

"We were brought to Xulon through a wormhole, and our chief science officer believed the temporal flux might bring about the fever. It had already sped up the symptoms of our brother who was in the grip of it. I know now those fears were correct. Since landing on this moon, I've experienced stirrings of the fever. It is only a matter of time before I am within its clutches and helpless to master my lust."

I swallowed, but my throat was parched. "What happens if you don't...find a mate."

Torst exhaled slowly. "We go mad." His face twisted for a moment. "No Taori has succumbed to the fever madness for a long time, however. We do everything in our power to prevent it."

I rocked back, taking in everything he'd told me. As fantastical as his story was, I believed him. Then I cocked my head as something occurred to me. "Did you say temporal flux?"

A weary grin teased the corner of his mouth. "I wondered if you would catch that."

Physics hadn't been my favorite subject at the academy, and truth be told, I'd barely skated through, but I remembered the definition of a temporal flux. "Are you telling me you traveled through time to get here?"

"According to our ship's systems before we were attacked, the wormhole brought us approximately five hundred astro-years into the future—and to a galaxy far from the one we were traversing."

I eyed the alien who'd been born generations before me. "Welcome to the future."

He choked back a laugh, smiling at me for a moment before frowning again. "So far, it holds little appeal."

"You mean because everyone is trying to kill you?" I returned his brief grin. "Everyone's a critic."

The alien choked back a gruff laugh. "You should get some sleep if we're going to find your friend and keep from being killed tomorrow. I'll take first watch."

Before I could argue with him, I yawned widely, slapping a hand over my mouth in embarrassment that the mere mention of sleep had provoked that. "Maybe just for a while."

Torst rose and left the cave, and I stretched across the back wall, curling onto my side, and using the crook of my arm as a pillow. My mind was whirring with everything that had happened and all that I'd learned, but as exhaustion overtook me and I drifted off, something he'd said teased the recesses of my mind. What was a mating clench?

CHAPTER
SEVENTEEN

Torst

Asnap made my eyes pop wide, and I was instantly on guard. Morning light peeked between the trees, the rushing water of the stream shimmering and the pearlescent rocks lining the banks gleaming brightly. I flinched from the sudden brightness, my eyes adjusting to not peering through the darkness.

The sound wasn't followed by another, so I allowed myself a hesitant breath as I took in the noises of the alien jungle. So far, I hadn't seen evidence of any large wildlife, but any environment with foliage and water would have insects and small creatures. The translucent, floating creatures with dangling tentacles spun through the air overhead along with the spiraling pink motes that were easier to see in the light. If there were birds, they stayed hidden—perhaps they were hunted once all the human prey was exhausted or maybe the floating tentacled creatures were the moon's version of birds, their shimmering, transparent bodies pulsing like beating hearts as they propelled themselves.

I swept my gaze around me, my tail twitching. I'd spent almost the entire night staring into the jungle, my acute vision searching for the mercenaries or a new Xulon hunting party. Part of me wished they'd returned so I could expend some of my pent-up energy in killing them. Another part of me—the reasonable side that was not burning with blood lust—was relieved that no one had happened upon our hiding place and that Lia had slept safely through the night.

I stood and rubbed the back of my neck, the bunched muscles aching from being on alert for so long. From the low angle of the light diffused through the hazy atmosphere, I could tell the sun—or suns—hadn't been up for long, but we couldn't let any more time slip through our fingers. Not if we wanted to stay ahead of the hunters.

"You didn't wake me."

I turned as Lia passed between the dangling vines and joined me. "You needed rest."

She frowned at this as she swept her silky, black hair up and fastened it so that it cascaded from the top like a sleek tail. "So did you."

I didn't tell her that I'd nodded off at some point close to dawn, or that I'd longed to join her in the cave. Not that she would have welcomed my presence after everything she'd learned about me. I should be grateful that she hadn't fled into the night.

"I hope you aren't going to argue about me coming with you to find Val." She folded her arms over her chest in challenge.

I shook my head. "Now that there are trained mercenaries on the hunt, it isn't safe for me to leave you, even in a well-hidden cave like this. You are with me."

"Good." She relaxed her stance. "Then we should probably get going."

Now that it was light again, I knelt and studied the ground around the cave. The undergrowth and soil were disturbed, but I suspected that was from our arrival and possibly the mercenaries passing by. There were no signs of something heavy being dragged, although if Lia's friend was even as remotely as slight as her, she would have been easy to carry.

"If Val had left on her own, she would have been limping," Lia said, "but I can't imagine why she would do that. She promised me she'd stay until I came back."

I didn't want to give voice to what we were both thinking. The human hadn't left alone—and it probably hadn't been by choice. "You didn't hear anything strange?"

"Like her screaming bloody murder as someone dragged her away?"

I peered up at Lia, her mouth scrunched to one side in obvious irritation. "I'll take that as a no."

She spread her arms wide as I stood. "I know I'm not some super tracker with night vision, but I don't see any signs of her limping from here or being killed. Even if she'd been shot by a bow, there would be some blood, right?"

I grunted. "Then we assume she was taken by someone who knew what they were doing. They were fast, and they didn't leave a trail."

Lia's face lit up. "Maybe it was one of my security force teammates. If they were also dropped here, maybe they found her."

"How many members of your team were also taken by the Xulonians?"

"Two—Carly and Jasmine. There are other females who were abducted from our ship, but they're scientists like Val—or passengers."

I didn't think it likely that her other friends had taken Val, but I didn't want to extinguish the flicker of her hope.

"If we find Val, maybe we'll find more of my friends."

I didn't respond, but I moved to the edge of the stream, scooping up a handful of water and drinking. The cool liquid was refreshing, so I drank a few more mouthfuls in hopes that it would fill my empty stomach until I could find food. Lia did the same, squatting down and cupping the clear water in her hands. Then she sat back and eyed the stream and muttered something about eels. "Whoever found her, they probably continued to use the water as cover. Tramping through the jungle is too loud and easy to track."

"Agreed." I gestured upstream. "We should continue the way you two were walking."

Lia lowered her feet into the water, sucking in air as the stream swirled around her ankles. "Come on in, smooth talker. The water's fine but beware of the eels."

I glanced at the burbling stream, seeing no evidence of eels. Was this some kind of human humor? I followed her into the bracing water and started trudging side by side with her up the stream. As we moved in silence, I slipped my blade off my waistband and held it in the hand farthest from her. The serrated battle blade of the Taori wouldn't shield us from arrows, but the feel of the cool handle comforted me.

The burning hunger that had torn through me last night was now dormant, and if I was a Taori who believed in delusions, I might have been able to convince myself it had been doused for good. But I knew the fever would return with excruciating intensity, growing more powerful every time I denied myself release.

The water sloshed around our legs, the sound mingling with the gurgling of the stream as it flowed over rocks and danced in spinning eddies. I chanced a look at Lia, but her attention was on placing her feet between the slippery rocks and holding her arms out for balance.

She hadn't mentioned the mating fever since we'd spoken of it last night, but there was no chance she'd forgotten about it. Then, again, what was there to say? There was one thing—one promise she needed to make me.

"When the time comes, I will tell you to run, and you cannot disobey me."

Lia's steps faltered, her arms wobbled, and she clutched my arm to keep from slipping into the water. "Wait, what? Do you see something? Did you hear something?"

I stopped and faced her, the stream flowing effortlessly around us. "You cannot be stubborn about this or challenge me. When the mating fever becomes uncontrollable, I will no longer be able to protect you. I will be a danger to you. You must promise me that you will run when I tell you."

She gaped at me, her lashes fluttering as she blinked rapidly. "I thought you said it would drive you mad."

I gave a half shrug. "There are those who would argue I'm half mad already."

"You're serious?"

"The Taori revolve around honor like the planets circle their star. Dishonor is worse than madness for an Immortal. If I hurt you, I would never be able to live with myself. I want to believe that I would be able to resist you, but I've only felt the early stirrings and already it took every bit of control not to claim you. Once the fever takes me, I don't trust my honor to win out over my primal urges."

"That might be the nicest and weirdest thing any guy has ever said to me."

I held her gaze intensely. "Do I have your word?"

"No."

I groaned and tipped my head to the heavens. "Did you hear nothing I said, female?"

"Oh, I heard all of it, but I don't think I could live with myself if I let you suffer. Not after you saved me from being killed and then vowed to go mad so I wouldn't be hurt."

I narrowed my gaze at her. "I don't understand."

She bit her bottom lip, which quivered softly. "You need to mate with a female, or you'll go mad. I'm willing to be that female."

I stared at her in disbelief. She was offering her body to me? She was giving herself to me to be claimed in a mating fever? Then I looked her up and down. She was too small, and the Taori mating frenzy was too intense. And then there was the fever clench. My face burned as I thought of her tiny body being anchored to me until the fever passed.

I pulled away from her, shaking my head violently. "I refuse your offer."

EIGHTEEN

Lia

Hot shame coursed through me, scorching my face and making my eyes burn as if on fire. What I'd said had been impulsive, and I'd doubted myself the moment the words left my lips, but when he turned me down, my mouth dropped. "I'm sorry, what?"

Torst's head was bowed as he shook it from side to side, as if attempting to shake his horns off. "I won't."

Thank the stars he wasn't looking at me, as tears nearly spilled from the corners of my eyes. I'd seen his gaze travel up and down my body after I'd offered myself, and then he'd firmly rejected me. Was I really that unappealing?

My throat was thick as I cleared it and forced myself to speak. "Are humans not compatible with the Taori?"

"They are, but I...cannot."

The flat-out rejection was like a slap to the face. Torst would rather go mad than fuck me. If I'd thought things were going badly for me before, this was an all-time low. I spun away from him, my vision blurry as the tears threatened to fall, and I powered forward through the water, not caring about slipping on the slick rocks or being bitten by eels. I would not let the alien see me cry or let him know much he'd hurt me with his outright rejection.

"Fine," I muttered, venom and pain dripping from my voice. "Go insane for all I care."

Behind me, he huffed out a loud breath and gave chase, his feet splashing as he caught up to me. My legs might not be as long as his, but I could be fast when I wanted to be—and right now, I wanted to put as much distance between myself and the Taori as possible.

What kind of male turned down an offer of sex, especially when it could save him? One who looked me up and down before deciding he didn't find me even remotely attractive, that's who.

I was aware that not everyone favored figures like mine that were short on curves, and I'd always felt self-conscious about my angular build and small breasts. There were few other humans of part Filipino descent on the colony where I'd been raised and none at the academy. How many times had I longed for the curves than men drooled over, or even the bouncy, curly hair that so many of my friends boasted? But my genetics had given me stick-straight hair and breasts that could generously be called a perky handful—if the hands weren't huge.

Even so, I'd been hit on enough times as an adult to almost forget the teasing I'd endured when I was growing up. Almost. Torst's rejection brought back all the snide comments from the mean girls who'd developed early and lorded their cleavage over those of us who had none. Suddenly, I was an insecure fifteen-year-old who would have rather gone through more treatments at the hospital than the brutal taunting in the school hallways because I'd looked different.

"Lia," he called out gruffly.

I ignored him. I didn't want to hear him attempt to apologize. I didn't want his pity or his half-assed excuses. The truth was it was only blind lust that could make him want me. If he wasn't being affected by his Taori mating fever, he wouldn't spare me a second glance. That had been abundantly clear when he'd refused my offer.

"Lia!" This time he grabbed my arm and spun me around before I could yank away. "Stop running from me."

I shook off his grip and glared at him, grateful that my hot tears had been replaced with indignant fury. "I'm not running. There's nothing to say. I tried to help you. You decided you'd rather go mad. Did I miss any of the high points?"

He grunted as he loomed over me. "You did not know what you were offering."

"So now I'm clueless as well as unappealing?" I wasn't even trying to keep my voice low anymore.

Torst's tail swished rapidly from side to side behind him. "I did not say that you were either."

"You didn't need to. For your information, I'm not some innocent girl, and I'm sure as hell not a virgin. If I decide to screw someone it's because I want to, and I don't need it mansplained—or in this case aliensplained—to me." I gasped in a quick breath. "And another thing, I'm a trained military officer who graduated at the top of my class, so the last thing I need is for you to tell me that I don't know what I'm doing."

His blue eyes never left mine, but they widened as my voice rose to a shrill peak. When he didn't respond to my outburst, I let out a groan of frustration and stomped away from him. One thing he had in common with all males—he was infuriating and short on words.

As much as I appreciated his help in finding my crewmate, I didn't know how I was supposed to work with him after this. Usually, rejection was followed by one or more of the parties avoiding the other, but we didn't have that luxury. I was stuck with the alien until we could find a way off the moon—or until one of us got killed.

That thought sobered me and deflated my indignant anger. Torst's mating fever might not even be an issue if the mercenaries or the new hunting teams found us, and my outburst hadn't helped.

"Ducking hell, Lia." I slowed my pace, bending and bracing my hands on my knees. Once again, I'd let myself be ruled by my emotions and the painful wounds that seemed to resurface at the worst times. My external scars were gone. When would the internal ones vanish? I let Torst catch up to me, swiveling my head to look at him as he bent over quickly, snatching an eel from the water, and tossing it so far it hit the water with a crack.

He stopped and towered over me, beads of sweat trailing down the star chart emblazoned across one chest muscle. "Are you ready to listen, or would you prefer screaming at me again?"

Ouch. "I deserve that. I shouldn't have freaked out at you. It's not about you—not really, but can we not talk about it?"

"But I need to tell you why—"

I pressed my lips together and shook my head. "I'd rather we focus on finding Val and keeping one step ahead of the hunters. I've already distracted us enough for one morning."

He frowned, growling low as I resumed walking up the stream, and he fell in step beside me, but to his credit, he didn't argue with me. Maybe we could get past this, I thought. Maybe we'd be able to pretend it had never happened.

Then an arrow whizzed by my ear.

I fell forward, putting a hand to my ear, which had been grazed by the arrow, and pulling back crimson-stained fingers. Then I looked up at Torst and the shiny, steel arrow lodged in his shoulder, blood already trickling down his tattooed bicep.

CHAPTER
NINETEEN

Torst

The pain was so sudden that it took me a heartbeat to register that I'd been struck by an arrow. Time seemed to slow as my body reverberated with the shock, even as another arrow sliced through the air and ruffled the hair by my ear.

"Get down!" Lia tugged at the leg of my pants roughly, her gaze fixed on the weapon protruding from my shoulder. An arrow skimmed over her head, even though she was bent low.

Gritting my teeth, I grabbed the arrow buried in my flesh and snapped off the long tail. Fresh waves of pain rolled through me, but I forced them aside. There would be time to roar later. Now, it was time to run.

I bent down and tossed Lia over my good shoulder, despite her squeals of protest. I could run faster than she could, and we needed to outrun this new group of hunters. I made sure her legs were hanging down my back as I took off through the water, holding her face to my chest with my uninjured arm.

From the direction the arrows were flying, the hunting party was on one side of the stream, but not close enough that I could see their red skin through the trees. *If* they were Xulonians, I thought, as my stomach knotted. I dismissed the possibility that the mercenaries had found us. If trained killers had attacked us, we'd already be dead. Mercenaries weren't bad shots, and any hunters who didn't get a kill after shooting so many arrows were bad shots.

Heartened by this, I picked up my pace, waving aside the floating tentacled creatures in the air as I reached the far bank of the stream and zigzagged around gleaming, ivory rocks to go deeper into the jungle. The arrows stopped flying around us, no doubt because the hunting party was making their way through the water. That, and we were more challenging targets as we weaved through the willowy trees and cascading vines.

"Put me down," Lia said, once there was only the sound of my footsteps crunching on the undergrowth. "I'm not the one who got shot."

I slowed and swung her down in a single motion, favoring my injured arm. "I'm not going to apologize. I needed to get us away from there fast."

She held up her palms. "I wasn't going to complain." Her gaze darted to the broken arrow wedged in my arm, and she bit her lower lip. "I was going to thank you. I panicked when I saw that you'd been shot. I don't know why. It's not like I haven't seen people get shot before, but a blaster shot isn't as gruesome as an arrow."

I allowed myself to look at the jagged metal in my shoulder. It was a hollow arrow, the metal not as rigid as I'd expected since I'd been able to snap it in half. Still, the head of it was no doubt pointed and impossible to remove without tearing through more flesh. Now that I wasn't moving, my mind focused on the throbbing pain and the blood trickling red down my darkly inked skin. The marks on my shoulder were thick swirls meant to depict the veil beyond this world—the one we would all one day move through to the shadowlands—and now the art would be marred. I growled in displeasure. At least I had no intent to journey to the actual shadowlands. Not yet, and not at the hand of alien hunters.

"How badly does it hurt?" Lia stepped closer and eyed the wound.

I grunted in response. I doubted my pain scale was the same as a human female's.

"We should bandage you up before you lose too much blood, or it gets infected." She fanned away some of the glimmering motes floating near my arm.

I grimaced at the thought of an infection but shook my head. "No time. We need to keep moving. The hunters aren't far behind us."

Lia craned her neck to peer over her shoulder. "Okay, but you're not carrying me."

I had no argument with that. The throbbing pain was making me lightheaded, and I wondered if the Xulonians used poisoned arrows. It would be just like the craven aliens to handicap their prey even further.

I did take her hand as I resumed running through the jungle. The foliage was thick, and I couldn't risk her falling behind. My stride might be longer, but she would keep up with me if she had to, even if that meant I partially dragged her.

We were still heading upstream, a direction I wanted to maintain since it was away from the hunting party and the mercenaries. There was always a chance we were running straight toward another group of hunters, but we'd have to take our chances. Better the wraith we knew than the one shrouded in mystery.

Blood continued to trail down my shoulder muscle, my swift movement increasing the flow and making my head swim. Spots danced in front of my eyes as I pushed aside large, lacey fronds, the tree trunks becoming more spread apart. After a while, I didn't know if I was imagining it or if the jungle was disappearing. Slats of light no longer peeked through a thick canopy of leaves overhead. It shone brightly on tall, feathery grass that had replaced the loamy soil tangled with foliage.

"I guess this moon isn't one big jungle," Lia said as we cleared the last of the towering trees and stepped into a wide field.

A rumble escaped my throat as I scanned the flat open land. Wind blew across the shimmering grass, and far on the horizon the ground appeared to drop off into a dark, churning sea. There was no place to hide here, and I glanced back longingly at the jungle.

Before I could pull us back, voices came from within the jungle—quickly approaching voices accompanied by thrashing footfall. We hadn't lost the hunters. They were closing in on us.

Lia jerked my hand as she started to move through the grass. "We can't go back now. We can only go forward."

I scowled at this but fell in step with her, racing across the field. She was right. As bad as this was, there was no other option.

As we approached the edge of the grasses, the brutal crash of waves met my ears. But we weren't running toward a beach or a smooth stretch of land leading into the sea. We were racing toward a rocky cliff.

"Duck me!" Lia skidded to a stop as the field ended abruptly, clods of dirt and pebbles flying over the side. "It's a dead end."

I peered over the edge, my throat tightening as I saw the roiling water below. I could only imagine what kind of creatures dwelled beneath such a deep, dark sea. I pulled back, looking in both directions. We could run farther ahead, but it appeared to be more open field, which would provide us no cover. Then there was the jungle behind us, but that was teeming with hunters.

When an arrow cut through the air between me and Lia, my decision was made for me. I clutched her hand and squeezed it. "You were right. We can only go forward."

Then I jumped off the cliff, taking the female with me and holding onto her small hand as if it was a lifeline.

CHAPTER
TWENTY

Lia

I opened my mouth to scream, but no sound came out as we plunged through the air toward the sea. I flailed the one arm that Torst wasn't holding, but the desperate motion did nothing to slow my descent. We were falling fast, and it was going to hurt like hell—if we survived.

Bracing myself for the hit and pointing my toes as much as possible, I gasped when my body knifed into the water. Instantly, I was swallowed by the frigid sea and sucked down by my momentum. Torst's hand was wrenched from mine, and he vanished into the darkness.

I hadn't been able to suck in a deep breath before hitting the water, so my lungs burned as I fought to find air. Opening my eyes didn't help. The water was nearly black, as it churned around me. Kicking with everything I had, I finally broke the surface and sucked in a greedy breath. There was no time for me to relish in my survival as waves battered me, crashing around me and on top of me as I struggled to stay above the water.

The shock of the cold numbed my limbs and had me gasping, but I kept kicking. For the first time in my entire life, I was grateful my parents had forced me to swim for rehabilitation. At the time I'd despised the mindless laps, but now it was that muscle memory that was keeping me alive. I scissored my legs wildly to propel my head above the rough sea, my gaze searching for Torst.

He'd been right beside me as we'd gone into the water, then he'd been ripped away. Was he still under the surface? I drew in a breath and ducked under, opening my eyes in a vain attempt to find him. If he was under there, I couldn't see him.

My heart raced as I returned to the surface, panic that he might have been killed in the fall or be drowning beneath me making my movements even jerkier.

"Calm down," I told myself. "You can't help him if you panic."

The swell continued to lift me up and down as white water bubbled. When a large swell popped me up like a cork, I spotted a flash of Torst's silvery horns. My pulse spiked. He was alive!

Almost as soon as I gave an internal cheer that he was okay, I realized that he wasn't. His wounded arm was making it impossible for him to swim or keep himself from being knocked under by the waves. His head barely crested the surface, and his face was tipped back as if he was trying to snatch breaths before going under.

Duckitty duck duck. I couldn't let him drown. Not after he'd saved me and kept me from being found by the mercenaries. Especially not after he'd taken an arrow for me.

I swiveled my head to take in our surroundings. We weren't on a wide-open field being pursued by hunters with bows anymore, but our prospects hadn't improved much. The cliff we'd jumped from rose straight into the air, jagged pearlescent rock creating a brilliantly bright wall—but there was no beach. The water crashed directly onto the rock face, and more jagged rocks jutted up from the water around me.

I uttered my versions of curses under my breath. "Where are we supposed to go now?"

Tilting my head up to the sky, I searched for the shiny, red faces of hunters peering over the side, but there were none. Either they were still in pursuit and hadn't reached the edge of the cliff or they'd seen us go over and left us for dead. If they knew what lay below the edge, I didn't blame them.

"It doesn't matter," I said, spitting out a mouthful of briny water. "He's not going to drown. Not on my watch."

I spun around and spotted Torst's horns again, powering my way through the water with practiced strokes until I reached him. As I'd thought, he was weak and losing his fight to stay afloat.

"Torst!" I called over the thrashing water. "I'm going to swim you in and keep your head above the water."

His eyes fluttered, and he rolled his head over to look at me. "Swim in where?"

"I don't know yet, but at least I can keep you from drowning while we figure out something." I ducked underwater and grabbed him by the waist, rotating him so he faced away from me and coming up behind him. I kicked hard to lift myself from the water as much as possible before throwing an arm across his uninjured shoulder and chest and pulling him flush to me.

I'd known he was big but keeping his body afloat along with my own was a stark reminder of just how much bigger he was than me. I fluttered my legs feverishly as the waves broke over both of us.

"Jumping off the cliff might not have been the best plan," he said, coughing out some water as he spoke.

I barked out a laugh and swiped at my eyes, which stung from the salt water. "Why would you say that? This is great. I'd been hoping for a vacation by the sea."

Torst grunted, but if I was getting better at deciphering his non-verbal sounds, it was an amused grunt. At least we would both die laughing.

After a few moments of bobbing together, my legs burning from kicking hard and fast enough to keep us both afloat and my one free arm weary from pulling through the water, he lifted a hand. "There."

I followed his leveled finger, my gaze scouring the rock. At first, I saw nothing. Then my eyes caught the uneven opening that looked low enough for us to crawl into. I couldn't tell from here if it was shelter, but at least it was above the crashing waves.

Just then, something large bumped my leg under the water. The sea was too dark and churned up for me to see what it was, but the large, pointed fin that skimmed the surface next to us removed any possibility that it had been Torst. And I had a feeling the creature wasn't bumping me to say a friendly hello. Duck duck duck.

I didn't think Torst had seen it—his eyelids were fluttering weakly, and his gaze was unfocused. Correction. I hoped he hadn't seen it. I only wanted one of us to panic at a time, and this was my time.

"Hold on," I told him, kicking us toward the rock ledge as fast as I could. Torst kicked as well, even though he couldn't paddle with his arms, and his long legs propelled us faster than my short ones could alone. As we got closer, waves pushed us forward, and I had to kick furiously not to get sucked back or slammed onto one of the rocks protruding from the water. I paddled with the arm not holding onto Torst, finally reaching the ledge, and slapping my hand onto it. "We're here. Hold on with one hand while I hoist you onto the rock."

Torst nodded, but didn't even utter a grunt, which worried me.

I glanced quickly behind us, catching a glimpse of the shining fin cutting through the water too close for comfort. I pivoted from under Torst and put his good arm onto the ledge before heaving myself from the water. Without stopping to catch my breath, I reached down and tried to pull him up. I tugged as hard as I could, but he was so much heavier above the water. I even grabbed one of his horns, but quickly realized that pulling him out by the head wouldn't work.

"Come on, Torst!"

He looked up at me just as I peered over him at the creature swimming toward us. It was skimming right under the water with its wide jaw open and lots of serrated teeth flashing. Why did everything on this moon seem to be so deadly?

He must have seen the fear on my face because he let out a determined growl, threw a leg up onto the ledge, and hurled himself up the rest of the way with an agonized roar. I sat back hard, water streaming down my face and body and puddling around me. Glancing up, I saw that the overhang shielded us from view. No one above could see us.

I scanned the water. The sea creature had turned back around, his attempt to eat Torst as a snack foiled.

I blew out a breath. For now, we were safe.

"We made it," I said, crawling over to Torst, who was lying on his back. Forget that we'd almost drowned and that my legs were on fire from kicking hard enough to keep the big lug afloat. My frigid skin went even colder when I saw that the momentum to get him onto the rock had pushed the arrow deeper into his flesh.

His eyes fluttered open for a moment before they closed, and his head slumped to one side.

TWENTY-ONE

Torst

A wave of contentment rushed over me as I peered up at her. The female straddled me, her hands braced on my bare chest and her thick, brown hair falling over her shoulders and brushing my skin. Her horns were smaller than mine, but the ridges within them contain hints of iridescent pink, reminding me of the inside of a borva shell. Her tail curled up behind her, swishing back and forth languidly, the rounded tip quivering slightly.

"You have no patience, Torst,"

I laughed, the sound bubbling up within my chest. "Me? Who is the one who refused to wait until after our bonding ritual?"

She swatted at me, although the strike was only in jest. "You wished to wait longer? The noises you made didn't sound like the sounds of a Taori who regretted his impatience."

I growled at this, grasping her naked hips and rolling her

over onto her back. "I have no regrets, but maybe I need to make sure you're pleased with your decision?"

She wrapped her legs around my waist and squeezed. "You know I was well-pleased, just like I will be every night in our furs when we're mates."

"Every night?" I gave her what I hoped was a wicked grin. "I will hold you to that promise, Kaolin."

She wiggled beneath me and licked her lips. "I would prefer you hold more to me than a promise."

A low rumble gathered in my core as I gazed upon the face of my intended, a face I'd known since we were children. My heart constricted as she smiled at me, even as fresh desire made my cock swell again. "There is no moment like this one."

Her smiled faltered, and her gaze darted behind me. "We've been gone long enough. Our families will wonder why we aren't helping with the preparations."

"My kinsman will not wonder where I am, nor will my fellow warriors. This ritual is only a formality. You know you're already mine, Kaolin. You always have been."

Her expression softened, then she cocked her head at me, shaking a finger. "You're as sly as you are charming, but you've sweet-talked me enough today, Torst."

She gave me a hard shove and pushed me off her. My intended might be a female, but she was strong. I fell off her and onto the hardpacked ground.

"The bonding ritual may be a formality, but it's one that means something to our clans." She pulled on her animal hide skirt and fastened the band around her breasts. "Even if it means nothing to a ravenous male like you."

I grabbed for her, but she danced from my reach. "It doesn't mean nothing to me. It means I won't have to sneak off beyond the borders of our city to take you." I stood and tugged on my own pants, brushing the dust off them. "It means I won't have rocks embedded in my ass after you ride me."

She pretended to be scandalized, spinning away and running toward the Taor city. I laughed and took off after her, our bare feet kicking up dirt behind us.

The terrain around us was rough and rocky, but that was merely a ruse. Once we reached the energy dome under which our modern city hid, everything would change, and the lifeless rocks and dry, cracked ground would become glittering spires and gleaming buildings. On Taor, the old melded with the new, and we honored our ancient ways while also embracing technology.

Kaolin's long legs ate up the distance between us and the city, and her lilting laugh drifted back to me as I ran behind her. I liked watching her run so much—her hair flying behind her—that I didn't bother to catch her. Since we were young, I'd always let her win when we raced, although now there was an incentive to catching her there'd never been before.

A pain in my arm made my steps falter, but when I glanced down at my bare bicep, there was no reason it should ache. I ignored it and turned back to Kaolin. Her form flickered, and I blinked a few times. We hadn't reached the energy dome, so why was she fading in and out? Another pain shot through my arm, and I gasped, touching my hand to the perfectly smooth flesh.

Before I could wonder what was happening to me, shadows darkened the ground between me and Kaolin. I glanced up, and my stomach plummeted. Dark beasts were flying toward us, claws and fangs bared.

I tried to scream, but my mouth wouldn't open. A blinding pain in my arm sent stars dancing across my eyes, blurring my view of my intended as she ran. Had she seen them yet? I called out a frantic warning, and she turned. In an instant, her teasing smile vanished, replaced by terror. She whipped back around and increased her pace, her legs pumping hard as she neared the energy dome.

What were these creatures? Taor didn't have predators like this. Were we being invaded? I looked to the skies again. If so, planetary defenses would be flying overhead.

Kaolin was so close to passing through the energy field that I exhaled in relief. Then one of the monsters snatched her, its cruel claws biting into her as it lifted her into the air. Her screams tore into my heart as the beast ripped her apart while I ran helplessly, my own screams taking over when hers ended.

"Torst!"

More pain in my shoulder as I was shaken. I opened my eyes, panting as I stared up at another female. Not Kaolin.

Slowly, the nightmare faded, and I remembered where I was. Far from the Taori home world, and a lifetime away from the first appearance of the Scythians—after the beasts had crawled from the caves within which they'd been festering and gathering strength for longer than we'd known. As my eyes focused on the rock overhang I was lying beneath, memories of the rough sea and being kept afloat by the female crept into my brain.

"Lia," I said, more to remind myself of her name. I tried to push myself up on my elbows, but she put a hand on my chest to keep me down.

"I wouldn't move yet." She gave me an apologetic look. "I had to pull that arrow from your shoulder. It was starting to look red and inflamed, and I wasn't sure if it was getting infected. There's so much weird stuff in the air here, I needed to close the wound."

I cut a glance to my shoulder. Instead of a shiny, metal rod protruding from the skin, it was wrapped in a swath of fabric and tied.

"I ripped off the bottom half of my shirt," she said, holding up the frayed hem. "I dipped it in salt water before wrapping your arm, so it's as clean as it can be, but I don't know what your tattoos are going to look like when it heals."

"That doesn't matter," I said, even though the markings that adorned my skin did tell a story, and having that tale marred felt like a loss. Still, I was alive, and I owed that to the human. "Thank you."

"I wouldn't say we're even, but we're getting there." She grinned at me. "I might actually owe you one after pulling that arrow from your arm. I was sure your screams were going to bring the cliff down on us."

My memory of the arrow being torn from my flesh was wrapped up in my memories of Kaolin's death, and my heart hadn't stopped pounding. It was as if I was still chasing after her. It had been so long since I'd dreamed of her, and so many long astro-years since she'd been killed, and I'd subsequently joined the mission to track down the Sythians and destroy them. The Torst in my memories, the male who'd been laughing and carefree, had died that day, replaced by a warrior bent on vengeance.

"I was worried about you for a bit," Lia said. "I thought you might already be feverish with an infection the way you were moaning and jerking."

I avoided her inquisitive gaze, not wanting to explain why I'd been thrashing, focusing instead on the alabaster ceiling of the rock overhang and releasing a pained sigh. "We're back in a cave."

She laughed, the sound echoing off the stone. "Looks like it, but it could be worse. The good thing about this cave is that I don't think those hunters can reach us unless they rappel or are excellent swimmers."

I was aware that the daylight had faded and the warm glow

of a setting sun—or two, since I hadn't gotten a good look at the solar situation—filled the shallow, wide-mouthed cave. I lifted my head to get a better look at the human, whose clothing was now torn and plastered wet to her body. "That also means our only way out is to climb up or swim."

Neither of which I'd be able to do for a while. I fought off the growing feeling of despair, reminding myself that Taori warriors did not quit. Death might beckon us with sweet whispers, but despair never would.

"Those aren't our only options." Lia shifted to one side and inclined her head to the darkest recesses of the makeshift cave, which extended farther back than I would have thought. "While you were out cold, I found a tunnel."

CHAPTER
TWENTY-TWO

Lia

Torst peered past me down the darkened, narrow tunnel that extended deeper into the rock. His eyes were barely focused, but he managed to prop himself up on one elbow for a better look. "So that's how we escape."

"Yes, but not now." I eyed his shoulder. "You're in no condition to move."

He scowled, and I braced myself for a grunt of protest, but one never came. "Even if I'm not at my full strength, we can't stay here for long."

I gave a cursory sweep of the open-mouthed cave created by the rock overhang, the salty spray of the sea water misting up as the waves struck the cliff. "I don't know. It might not be where I'd want to build a summer home, but it's not bad."

He tilted his head at me. "Summer home?"

"Old Earth humor," I said, forcing a laugh. "I watched a lot of vintage Earth movies when I was sick."

His confused frown deepened. "Sick?"

I glanced away from him, not wanting to see pity on his face when he learned how weak I'd once been. I busied myself wringing the water from my dripping ponytail. "As a kid. They didn't know if I was going to make it for a long time, but I did, and now I'm fine."

Neither of us spoke for a moment. If he was waiting for me to elaborate, he was out of luck. I'd done enough sharing for one day. It was hard enough to admit that I'd ever been ill, much less go into the details of my painful treatments and the constant shadow of fear that had defined my childhood.

Torst nodded, finally bestowing one of his guttural grunts on me. "And you chose to become a soldier?"

"Why not?" I hadn't meant to snap, but I didn't like the implication that I couldn't hack it because I'd been ill. "You don't think I'm up to the job?"

"What I think shouldn't matter," the Taori said slowly. "I'm not your superior officer."

"Damn straight, you're not," I said, more to myself than to him. But for some reason, it did matter to me what he thought. As much as I hated to admit it, he was a brave warrior and a smart soldier.

Torst sank back down onto the rock floor. "Now I understand why you're so fierce and determined."

Before I could say something snarky in return, I caught my breath. "You think I'm fierce?"

"You managed to get me from the water without drowning either of us. Then you pulled the arrow from my arm. Both took strength and grit. More than I'd have expected from a human female."

"Maybe you haven't met enough human women."

"You're correct. I've only encountered two before you, but

119

neither was a soldier, and I don't know if they would have been able to save me like you did."

I grinned at this, the compliment warming my cheeks. "It's a toss-up which was harder, keeping you from drowning or removing the arrow. You were thrashing and yelling a lot. I'm assuming 'Kaolin' is a Taori curse word? You yelled that over and over."

His expression darkened, and his eyes shuttered. Maybe the memory of the pain was coming back to him. "You also circle honor and bravery like the planets."

I smiled at this, murmuring, "Smooth talker." Then I thought of my friend and security force colleague, Carly, who was much braver than me, and my heart constricted. Where was she now? Where were any of the other women? My mind went to Val, and all my pride at having saved Torst evaporated.

I hadn't saved *her*. Where the hell had the scientist gone, and how was I supposed to find her while I was being hunted?

I distracted myself by moving closer to Torst and inspecting his bandaged wound. He flinched when I peeked under the fabric but didn't make a sound.

I, however, gasped loudly. "Holy turdballs!"

Torst's brow furrowed. "You consider balls of excrement to be worthy of worship?"

"It's an expression." I waved off his confusion, as I leaned closer to the torn flesh that was quickly knitting itself back together. "I'm shocked that you're healing so fast."

He didn't appear startled by this. "The Taori recover quickly from injury. It is another reason we were called the Immortal Army. It is rare for us to be felled for long."

"Must be nice." I gingerly replaced the makeshift bandage.

"I will not require much more rest." He glanced at me. "Not that I don't approve of this as a resting spot, but we will soon need food and water."

The mere mention of food made my stomach rumble, and I touched a hand to it. "If there is any. I didn't notice any edible berries or fruits in the jungle, and animals seem thin on the ground. I don't want to be picky, but I'm not eating those floating jellyfish things."

"They do not make it easy to survive out here if you manage to outrun the hunters, but it is a functioning environment, so there has to be something."

I wasn't sure if I agreed with him or trusted the Xulonians not to have stacked the deck significantly in the hunters' favor. It was already an uneven matchup with the prey having no weapons, but I didn't think they pretended to be hosting a fair fight. Not for the first time since I'd been dumped on the moon, I wanted to find the aliens who'd bought me from slavers and make them pay.

"Lia?"

I jerked my attention to Torst, who was gazing up at me intently. "Sorry. I was thinking of ways to kill the Xulonians."

A grin quirked up one side of his mouth. "First we find food and water. Then I will help you come up with many ways."

I gave a curt nod of agreement. "But before we take out the Xulonians, we find Val."

"And my Taori warriors, if they crashed on this moon."

I let out a growl of my own. "Then we go after the aliens who put us here."

Torst pushed himself up again. "Like I said, you are fiercer than most human females."

I swiveled toward the shadowy opening of the tunnel, my breath stuttering in my chest at the darkness that lay beyond. "Not fierce enough to want to go first into that."

"Do you fear what you cannot see?"

"Of course, I fear what I can't see. I can't see it!"

This brought a deep, sonorous chuckle from the Taori as he

got to his feet. "There is nothing to fear in the darkness, just as there is nothing to fear beyond the veil in the shadowlands."

"You mean death?" I narrowed my gaze at him. "Yeah, I'm not crazy about the uncertainty of that, either."

He closed his big hand around mine, heat pulsing up my arm. "Do not worry, female. I will lead the way."

As we stepped closer to the tunnel, me tucked slightly behind him, a strange rumble of voices came from the darkness. The tunnel wasn't empty.

I cut my gaze to Torst, whose body had tensed. "You're still sure about that?"

CHAPTER
TWENTY-THREE

Torst

I hesitated, placing a hand on the rock. My arm no longer ached, but I kept the fabric wrapped around it and used my other arm to sense the vibrations of the voices through my fingertips. I'd been trained to track on the Taori home world, although it had been a while since I'd practiced.

"They aren't close," I whispered to Lia. "These tunnels extend deep into the cliff."

"How do we know they come out again?"

I considered lying to the human to reassure her but decided against it. "We don't. We can only hope to the ancients that this is a way out."

"And how can you be sure those aren't Xulonian voices? Or the mercenaries sent to hunt us down?"

I twisted my head to look down at her. "I don't, but the red-skinned aliens I heard spoke with more clicks."

She held her breath as she listened to the low rumbling

echoing up to us. "You're right. That doesn't sound like the Xulonian I heard, either. It could be the mercenaries, but if that's the case, I think we can take them."

Once again, the small creature surprised me with a ferocity that didn't match her stature. "Then we continue?"

She eyed the tunnel warily before answering. "Duck, yeah."

I was growing accustomed to her strange expressions and fondness for waterfowl. I reached for her hand, closing my larger one around it. "So we do not get separated."

Her hand twitched in mine, but she didn't pull away. Warmth filled my chest. Not the burning, prickling heat of mating fever, though. It was a comfortable heat that suffused my body and made my pulse quicken. I exhaled in relief that I would not be walking into a dark tunnel with the urge to flatten Lia against the rock wall and hike her leg up around my waist. Of course, I wouldn't mind doing that either.

I shook my head and gave a grunt before trudging forward and pulling her with me. Within the first few steps, darkness consumed us. My vision shifted so that I saw shades of gray instead of the immersive blackness, but I kept my free hand on the wall as a guide, taking careful steps and breathing in the air as it grew stale and damp.

As I'd suspected, we were descending deeper into the cliff-side. I wasn't afraid of darkness or tight spaces, but I worried about what would meet us at the end. Was I leading Lia straight to the mercenaries? Was the tunnel a trap intended to lure us?

I forced those thoughts from my mind. There was no other choice if we wanted a chance to survive and find our shipmates. Climbing up the rock face of the cliffs would have been impossible, and it would have brought us back to the open field where we would have been picked off easily. The tunnel, as potentially treacherous as it might be, was our only option.

The voices that had been echoing from below had stopped,

and now the only sound filling the tunnel was our rhythmic breathing. When the tunnel slanted sharply and I slid forward a bit, Lia's hand almost slipped from mine, but I tightened my grip as I righted myself, and she emitted a gasp.

"Are you okay?" I asked once we were both steady again.

"I'm okay."

I couldn't see her as clearly as in the light, but her face was imprinted in my mind, her lovely, brown eyes tilting up as she smiled and wisps of her black hair framing her face. Her determined voice didn't match her beauty or her small body, but I'd seen for myself how hard she could push herself, and I would never doubt her again.

"How much farther do you think until the tunnel starts angling toward the surface?" she asked before we resumed walking.

I had no idea where the other end of the tunnel would emerge—in the jungle or in a part of the moon we'd yet to see —but I heard the quiver in her voice and remembered how cautiously she'd appraised the dark. "Not much farther."

She squeezed my hand. "Then let's do this."

I led us forward until I spotted the slightest glimmer of light ahead. It was more of a lessening of the complete darkness than anything, but before long, a warm glow reached us.

Lia released a sigh as the warm light grew stronger, and I glanced back at her pensive face. When she met my gaze, she grinned, although apprehension remained behind her eyes.

I turned back around, aware that, as welcome as the light was, it also meant that we would soon lose the protection of the darkness. Whatever voices we'd heard were at the other end of the tunnel, and it seemed like we were fast approaching that.

I dropped my hand from the stone wall and curled it around the hilt of my blade tucked in my waistband, pulling it out and holding it in front of me as we continued forward. Lia's hand tensed in mine, as if she was also bracing for whatever lay ahead.

As tough as I now knew she could be, there was no way I could suppress my desire to protect her. I moved my arm so that she was tucked behind me, as I detected the rustle of movement ahead.

I was poised to spring forward and attack as we rounded a bend, but I came to an abrupt halt and Lia bumped into me. Instead of red-skinned aliens with bows or mercenaries with blasters, we'd walked upon a group of shabbily dressed aliens gathered in a wide opening within the tunnel.

"Who are you?" I asked, my gaze roaming over the group in a vain search for any Taori.

"We're the same as you," an alien with long limbs and light purple skin said as he stood and eyed my blade, the antennae over his eyes swaying, "survivors of the hunt."

CHAPTER
TWENTY-FOUR

Lia

I stepped from behind Torst to get a better look at the small group. They'd all stood when we'd come around the corner, shuffling closer together. All except the one near the middle with his hands outstretched as he cupped a ball of fire that gave off no smoke.

So, that was where the light came from. We hadn't reached the surface at all. The hard knot of worry in my gut relaxed a bit as I realized there were no aliens or mercenaries waiting to kill us.

"Survivors of the hunt?" Torst asked, not dropping his defensive stance or his blade. "How is that possible?"

The alien who'd spoken smiled at Torst then at me. "The Xulonians used to be much worse at hunting than they are now."

"And they made the mistake of procuring prey who had talents to defend themselves," the creature holding the fire said, shifting the flaming orb from one hand to the other, as he eyed Torst. "I'm surprised they brought you here. You look like you could put up a fight."

"They didn't," Torst said. "I crashed onto the moon in an escape pod after the Xulonians destroyed my ship."

There were nods and murmurs all around.

"I was bought from slavers as prey," I said, after a few of the creatures snuck curious glances at me. "I'm human."

"They like humans." The alien with lavender skin gave me an apologetic look. "No offense to you, but your kind doesn't possess extraordinary strength or powers. You're easier to catch and kill."

The alien rolling the flames between his hands winked at me. "They didn't like it when I threw fire balls at them."

"Or when I used telekinesis to rip the weapons from their hands," a short creature with brown skin and spiky bumps covering his head added, after clearing his throat.

I touched a hand to Torst's arm, a gentle signal for him to lower his blade. He glanced at me and then at the weapon he still held outstretched, lowering it quickly as if he'd forgotten he was even holding it. "I'm Lia, and this is Torst. Like I said, I'm human, but he's Taori."

The lavender alien tipped his head forward, and his antennae bobbled. "I am Zennen from the planet Nanool."

The alien holding the fire lifted one flaming hand to his face, illuminating his vivid, green eyes and mess of straw-colored hair that made him look like any of the wild teenagers I'd known in the past. "Rafe."

The rest of the half dozen aliens introduced themselves, but the only other name that stuck out in my mind was Baboo, the name of the spiky-headed creature who could move objects with his mind.

I swept my gaze around the wide, round area, noticing for

the first time that there were multiple alcoves draped with rough fabric and more than one tunnel extending away. "So, you escaped being killed and ended up living down here? How do you survive underground?"

"Slowly and over time, those of us who avoided being hunted made our way into the tunnels," Zennen said, motioning for us to sit on one of the dry logs or hefty stones that served as seats.

Rafe swirled the fire in his hands and placed it on the stone in the center of the makeshift chairs, the dancing flames sending more shadows bouncing across the alabaster rock. Torst waited for me to sit before choosing the log next to mine, even though the wood creaked when he sat on it.

"Apologies." Splotches of pink appeared on Zennen's cheeks and the palms of his hands. "We aren't used to creatures as large as you. As I mentioned before, the Xulonians do not bring aliens they believe will be a genuine threat."

Torst grunted. "I am surprised they continued with the hunt if you all took out many of their citizens. Why would anyone wish to come to a hunt in which they could be killed?"

Baboo flicked his wrist and a log slid over to him. "The Xulonians don't die."

I exchanged a glance with Torst. "I saw this guy take down more than a few of them. Trust me, they aren't so tough without their bows and arrows."

"Baboo means that you killed their dimensional incarnation," Zennen said. "The actual Xulonians are still safe on their home world."

"Dimensional incarnation?" I looked around the fire at the solemn faces, the words tickling a memory in the back of my brain. Hadn't the mercenaries outside the cave mentioned those same words? "Do you mean avatars? The red-skinned creatures we're running from are only avatars?"

Rafe snapped his fingers. "Got it in one, sweetheart."

Torst growled and slid his gaze to Rafe, who smiled even wider.

I ignored Torst and Rafe, turning my attention back to Zennen. "Are you telling me it doesn't matter how many of them we kill, they don't really die, and more avatars will come after us?"

"I'm afraid so. They're highly xenophobic and agoraphobic, so even leaving their home world for one of their moons would be unthinkable for the average citizen."

"Cowards," Torst said, the word so low it was like a rumbling undercurrent.

"Exactly," Rafe said, shifting his mischievous smile to me. "Your guy might be quiet, but he's not slow."

Before I could explain that Torst wasn't necessarily my guy, and that we'd been thrown together by our mutual desire to stay alive, the Taori leaned forward and braced his elbows on his knees. "Are there any Xulonians on this moon?"

Zennen nodded. "There is a skeleton administrative team in a central command building. The director of the hunt stays there along with enough staff to ensure the dimensionals are functioning. They also retrieve any damaged ones and repair them."

Torst locked his gaze on Zennen. "Then there must be ships to take them back to the home planet."

"We see ships come and go," Baboo said before Zennen could respond. "We don't stay underground all the time."

"You must have to go to the surface for food," I said. "What kind of food is on this moon anyway? We haven't seen much worth eating since we've been here."

Furtive glances were exchanged around the fire.

Torst clasped his hands together in front of him. "If you're about to tell us you've eaten the rest of the survivors, this isn't going to end well—for you."

Rafe laughed out loud, his fingers sending off sparks that made everyone jerk back. "That's a good one. We're not cannibals, my Taori friend, but we are thieves."

"Explain," Torst said gruffly.

Zennen straightened and cleared his throat, making it clear he wanted to tell us. "You see these tunnels that go off in different directions?"

I darted a glance at the offshoot tunnels and nodded.

"We created them. Originally, there was a single tunnel that ran from the cliffside near the sea to the surface far away from here. I was the first creature to come down here, but once Baboo joined me, we were able to use his ability to move matter to create more tunnels and make a bit of a home down here."

Baboo grinned sheepishly. "We had to be careful not to weaken the rock and bring the entire cliff down on us, but I was able to create multiple ways for us to move around the moon without being seen. Some parts of the moon have natural tunnels. The rest, I created. I also accidentally tunneled up under the storage building for the Xulonian staff, so we take our food and supplies straight from them."

"We have to be careful, of course," Zennen added quickly. "We never take too much to be missed."

Torst made a gruff noise of approval. "It is the least the craven aliens deserve."

Rafe thumped the spike-headed alien on the back. "Baboo is a genius."

"And Rafe made it possible for us to have heat and light without creating smoke," Baboo said.

Rafe flicked his pointer finger, and a tiny flame erupted from it. "It's the least I could do after Zennen found me and brought me underground."

"So, you do try to save those put on the moon to be hunted?" I asked, hope blooming fresh within me.

Zennen's gaze dropped. "It's been harder now that the Xulonians are buying human slaves. The prey doesn't last long enough on the surface for us to find them."

"Those avatars have gotten better with a bow," a female alien with long, white hair said in a near whisper. "I think the same citizens come here again and again to improve their kill score."

I swallowed a sour taste in my mouth, trying to convince myself that Val was not part of someone's high score. "One of my human shipmates is still out there." I glanced at Torst. "There could be more, but I'm not sure where all the women from my ship were taken."

The white-haired female drew in a sharp breath and wouldn't meet my gaze as she worked her gloved hands together. "The prey is put in the jungle. If any other humans were put on this moon, they would be there."

So, chances were good only Valeria and I were dumped on the hunting moon. I was both relieved and sad.

"And I suspect at least one of my fellow Taori warriors crashed here, as well," Torst said. "I intend to find them both."

"Returning to the surface means death," Zennen said.

Torst rolled back his shoulders. "Death is a more welcome friend than dishonor."

TWENTY-FIVE

Torst

"We've never had a Taori here." Rafe gave me an appraising look. "Now I know why."

"I can't allow anyone under my protection to be harmed," I said, glad his attention had shifted to me and away from Lia. "And I can't permit these Xulonians to continue operating a hunting moon."

"What do you plan to do?" Zennen asked.

I readjusted myself on the hard log. "First, I'm going to find Lia's shipmate. Then I'm going to locate any other Taori stranded on this moon." I twisted my neck until it cracked. "Then I'm going to take out this hunting operation and make these Xulonians regret ever victimizing other creatures."

"Now that's what I'm talking about." Rafe reached over and shook my arm, his fingers like embers. "Someone who understands revenge."

"One correction to that plan." Lia nudged me with her elbow. "I'm going with you to find my shipmate. You're not leaving me behind."

I cut her a glance and growled low.

"Haven't I already proved that I'm tough?" She said before I could voice my protest. "Didn't I haul your ass from the sea when you were about to drown? Didn't you say how much stronger I was than you expected?"

"All of that is true," I grumbled, holding up a hand. "But that doesn't mean you should risk your life on the surface again. You did not fare well when being chased by hunters, and there are bound to be even more now."

"He is right," Zennen said, steepling his hands in front of him as his antennae quivered. "Those without extraordinary strength or powers do not survive up there. If you've cut down some of their dimensional incarnations, they will be sending out even more. The citizens who choose to spend their credits hunting other aliens do not like to lose."

"Then we have one thing in common." I fisted my hands and imagined killing more of their shiny-skinned avatars.

"And don't forget the mercenaries," Lia said. "You won't only be fighting untrained Xulonians this time."

"You don't think I could take some mercenaries?" There were few species as powerful and well-trained as the Taori, and I doubted five hundred years had changed that.

Lia rolled her eyes. "Not on your own you can't. You don't even have a blaster, and who knows what kinds of weapons they have?" She turned away from me, her long tail of hair whipping around and hitting my shoulder. "Just because you're a badass, doesn't mean I should let you do all of this on your own."

"He won't be on his own," Rafe said, rocking forward and

jiggling one leg. "I'd love a chance to fry up some more Xulonians."

"Did you say there were mercenaries?" Zennen asked.

I nodded. "Whoever oversees this hunt knows I'm here—or suspects it. Their kind destroyed my battleship, but a lot of my crew escaped in pods. I am not sure if they tracked our pods or if they figured out something was wrong when the human females took out an entire hunting party."

"Which could have happened if I'd had a laser rifle," Lia muttered.

Zennen tipped his head back and his antennae followed. "So, the surface is teeming with trained killers?"

I was sorry that my presence meant more danger for these survivors, but it couldn't be helped. The Xulonians would continue to hunt for me—and any other Taori down here—until we were eliminated. They had their twisted hunt to preserve and their citizens to entertain. "Which is why I need to launch an attack at the command center. Their attempts to track me down put all of you in danger."

Baboo stood, which didn't make him reach much above my head when I was sitting. "I'll help you. You might need more than your big muscles to take down the Xulonians."

I could not help but admire the small alien's courage. "I can't let you do that—or any of you. I'm the reason the mercenaries are here, and your safety is at risk. I need to take care of this myself."

Lia muttered something that sounded like "stubborn duck," while Rafe scowled at me, and Baboo looked hurt.

"You said you arrived here on a battleship," Zennen said. "Is that correct?"

I nodded, not knowing where this was going.

"Did everyone on this Taori battleship only do things to benefit themselves, or did you work as a team?"

I huffed out an impatient breath. "That is not the same thing."

"It's exactly the same thing." Lia stood to face me with her small hands balled into fists. "You told me that your fighters are called the Immortal Army. I doubt a member of the Immortal Army would insist on a solo mission when he had a team of fighters ready and willing to help." She locked her gaze on mine. "This isn't only your fight, Torst. We all have a reason to take down these Xulonian duckwads." She waved a hand at the other aliens around the fire. "These guys even more than us since they've been here longer."

"Your girl is right." Rafe spun a small ball of fire in the palm of his hand as he stared into it. "We deserve to be a part of your mission."

I frowned, even though my pulse quickened when he called Lia mine. Heat swirled in my core, sending familiar longings through me, followed by cold fear. If the mating fever was back, I didn't have long until I wouldn't be able to think clearly enough to plan an attack mission.

Turning to Zennen, I narrowed my gaze. "You approve of this?"

He shrugged. "I maintain that going to the surface is deadly, but it also seems that you have no choice. We have only survived this far by working together. I don't see a reason to change that now. You might have stumbled upon us, but you are as much a survivor as any of us. You are part of our family now." He pinned me with an intense gaze. "And we do not abandon family."

My throat was thick as I nodded. It would be dishonorable for me to reject their help—and it would be foolish. "Thank you."

Zennen stood. "It has been decided, but we cannot do

anything until we have rested. We were about to go to sleep when you arrived."

Now that he mentioned sleep, the weight of the day cascaded over me like a heavy shroud. Even though my arm was almost healed, the regeneration process had taken a lot from my body, draining me of energy and making my eyes heavy.

"We have an empty alcove you can share." Baboo nodded his head toward one of the curtained areas. "We were able to steal bedding from the Xulonians, but not mattresses. Those we made from stuffing dried grass between stitched up sheets. I hope you won't be too uncomfortable."

I followed his gaze to the alcove that had a lumpy mattress lying directly on the stone topped with a few worn, gray blankets. One mattress.

"I'm sure it will be fine," Lia said quickly. "It's generous of you to welcome us like this." Her voice broke. "It's been rough since we got here."

The female with white hair, who'd introduced herself as Yara, pressed her gloved hands to her cheeks. "You must be famished. Have you eaten since you've arrived?"

Another alien jumped to his feet, emitting a series of high-pitched clicks as he waddled over to another alcove and returned with two brown boxes and two shiny pouches. He handed a set to me and one to Lia, smiling to reveal pointy teeth that glinted like knives.

"The Xulonians eat lots of prepackaged meals," Rafe explained as I opened my box. "Either they don't keep a cook up here, or they like things in neat little boxes, but most of what we get is like this."

"Are you kidding?" Lia tore the cover off her box. "This is amazing. I'm used to military rations, which look way less appealing than this."

I was too hungry to even contemplate complaining—or adding my own gratitude to Lia's. If it was edible, I was eating it. I snatched a thick, dark stick and took a bite. Hard and chewy, but savory.

Rafe laughed, dragging a hand through his pale hair and sparks flying above his head. "You two really were hungry, weren't you?" He stood. "I won't make it weird by watching you eat." Then he stood and gave me a wicked grin, flitting his gaze to the single bed in our alcove. "Sleep well."

I swallowed hard as the rest of the aliens joined Rafe in adjourning to their own alcoves. The thought of sharing a bed with Lia sent a pulse of desire through me, but I didn't know if it was the mating fever or my growing awareness of how lovely she was—and how brave. I took a swig from the pouch of water. "I'll take the floor."

CHAPTER
TWENTY-SIX

Lia

I woke with a start, sitting up and looking around me. It only took a few moments for me to remember where I was—in the tunnels sleeping in an alcove with Torst. Well, not *with* Torst. He'd insisted on taking the floor, even though I'd told him there was room on the lumpy mattress. I shifted, and the dried grass crackled beneath me. Come to think of it, maybe he was smarter to take the floor. Grass didn't make the softest filling.

I scanned to where Torst had been stretched out beside the mattress, and my breath stuttered in my chest. He wasn't there anymore. Tossing back the scratchy blanket, I jumped up. If he'd snuck out without me, I was going to kill him—once I tracked him down and made sure the hunters weren't doing just that.

Sleep blurred my eyes, and I rubbed them as I staggered from the alcove, cursing creatively under my breath, and hoping he didn't have too much of a head start on me. When I reached the circular area where the ball of fire still burned on the rock floor, I stopped short. "Torst?"

He stood naked with his back to me at the mouth of one of the tunnels that extended in the opposite direction of the sea. I was both grateful that he hadn't gotten far and furious that he'd tried to ditch me—actually, all of us—after agreeing that we'd go after the Xulonians together. I was also confused as to why he was stark naked. If he was trying to ditch us, doing it naked was a bad plan.

I forced myself not to focus too much on his firm, round ass, or the tail that sprouted from right above it. Now that he no longer wore his leather pants, I could see that his dark tattoos swirled over every bit of him. The alien had looked good with clothes on, but this was next level.

"What the duck are you doing?" I whispered so I wouldn't wake up the others. "I know you weren't planning on running off to be a hero while the rest of us were sleeping—or doing it in the nude."

He didn't answer, and it was then that I noticed his hands in tight fists by his side and his arms trembling. What was going on?

Torst?" I said as I took tentative steps toward him. I touched his arm lightly when I reached him, and he jerked away as if my hand had scalded him.

"Don't touch me." His rough whisper cracked with pain.

"Is it your wound?" I looked at his shoulder, which was no longer tied with the hem of my shirt, but I could only see the back of it and not the torn flesh. I should have checked it before I fell asleep, but I'd been so exhausted that it hadn't occurred to me that his cut might get infected during the night. "If it's hurting, I can try to—"

"It's not my wound," he snarled, turning quickly to face me.

140

I stumbled back as he loomed over me, my gaze going to his injured shoulder, which looked miraculously healed. I desperately wanted to look lower, but my eyes were drawn to his searing gaze, and my mouth went dry.

The incandescent blue of Torst's eyes had been swallowed up entirely by the jet-black pupils which seemed to burn from within. His bare chest heaved, sweat trailing down his hard, darkly inked muscles, and heat rolled off his body as if he'd run a race. "You need to get away from me, and I need to leave before I... "

My heart pounded, but I refused to run from him. If this was the mating fever, then it had gotten worse. He looked like he was on the verge of snapping, his entire body vibrating from the effort of holding himself back. Even his tail was stiff behind him, as if he was willing every part of him to be still. "If you leave, you'll die. You said yourself that the fever will drive you mad, and I don't give a disoriented Taori in the throes of mating fever good odds against the hunters and mercenaries."

He gave a rough shake of his head, his hair swishing around his head. "That's better than..."

His words stung. This rejection was starting to do a number on my ego, but I tried to shake off the hurt. Behind me, someone shifted on one of the grass-filled mattresses, so I dropped my voice even lower. "You'd really rather die or go insane than be with me?"

His molten eyes widened, and he rolled his head as if trying to restrain himself. "You think I don't want you?"

"Um, yeah. You've basically said that you'd rather die than sleep with me." I held up two fingers. "Twice."

A soft growl rumbled from deep inside him, and he squeezed his eyes closed for a beat. "This has nothing to do with how much I want you." His eyes flew open, pinning me with a tortured gaze. "And I do want you, Lia. But I would rather die than hurt you, and I don't know if a human as small as you could survive the Taori mating frenzy."

My mouth gaped a bit. He wanted me? "I don't repulse you?"

His brow furrowed as he reached a shaky hand out to touch my hair, which I'd pulled from my high ponytail and now fell across my shoulders. "Since I first inhaled the scent of you, I've wanted you," he husked, each world stilted, as if it was painful to speak. "You are as intoxicating to me as the most potent Darillian whiskey, and more breathtaking than a Taori sunset over the mountains."

I stared up at him, finally exhaling a whoosh of breath when I realized I'd been holding it. "I had no idea...I thought... When I offered myself earlier you seemed so angry about it."

He clenched his jaw and pulled back his hand. "You don't know what you're offering. You still don't."

I glanced over my shoulder. "If the others wake up, you'll have to explain that you can't go after the Xulonians or help save them because you've chosen to go mad instead." He glowered at me, but I took his burning hand in mine. "I promise you that you won't hurt me."

Then I stole a glance at the enormous cock jutting out from his body, and I almost changed my mind. Not only was it thick and long, but it also had a series of three bulbous crowns down the length of it. I gulped. This called for the real words.

Fuck me.

CHAPTER
TWENTY-SEVEN

Lia

I pushed back the coarse fabric curtain to the alcove and pulled him inside, letting the fabric fall partially over the opening, so that only a sliver of light from the central fire peeked into the private sleeping area. It wouldn't do much to muffle sounds, but it would give us some privacy. My heart was hammering, and my palms were damp, and whatever confidence I'd felt moments earlier evaporated now that I was standing alone with Torst.

Did I really know what I was doing, or was this another case of me trying to prove myself by being reckless? I shook this thought from my mind. My mother's warnings were the last thing I wanted to be remembering right now.

Torst towered over me in the small space, his head brushing the stone ceiling. He turned me to face him, his hands still shaking as he held me by the arms. "It isn't too late for me to leave. You can still say no, and I can run away from here."

Every word seemed to be ground painfully from his mouth, his self-control barely holding him back.

Tilting my head up so I could see the shadows of his face in the faint light, I swallowed down any remnants of fear. The Taori might be impressively big everywhere—and his tiered cock gave me serious pause—but I wanted this. I wanted him. And it wasn't only because it would save him from the fever. I was drawn to the primal power of him but also the fierce tenderness that wanted to protect me—even from himself.

I ran a hand across his chest, letting the pulsing heat of his flesh brand me. "I don't want you to run away from me." I leaned closer to him, my lips almost brushing his skin as both nerves and desire consumed me. "I want you to fuck me."

My words snapped something inside him because he moved so quickly, I didn't have time to breathe before he'd crushed his mouth to mine, one large hand palming the back of my head as he flattened me against the wall. His kiss was urgent, his tongue parting my lips quickly as his hands tugged roughly at my clothes.

Shockwaves of desire pounded through me as my heartbeat spiked. He tasted as dark and dangerous as I'd imagined, but his lips were surprisingly soft for someone so deadly. I hadn't expected his kiss to unravel me, his lips moving against mine and his tongue stroking mine as if a prelude for what was to come.

When he tore his mouth from mine, his words were husky and needy, and his dark eyes glittered with a barely contained frenzy. "I can't go slow. I need to be inside you." He bent and ran his face up the length of my neck, inhaling deeply as he did so. "But I also need to taste you."

I didn't have time to ask if this was part of his fever before he was dropping to his knees and yanking down my pants.

When they were around my ankles, I stepped from them, and he hitched one of my legs over his shoulder.

There was nothing gentle about the way he parted me with his hot tongue, lapping wildly like he was devouring me.

"So wet," he growled, his lips buzzing my slick flesh, "and so sweet. Just like I imagined your sex would taste."

The idea that he'd been imagining how I would taste made me whimper, and the needy sound reverberated through the alcove along with his low growls. When his tongue found my clit, I gasped and clenched my hands on his horns for balance. He seemed to like this, growling louder, the vibrations making me suck in a sharp breath.

"Do you like me touching your horns?" I whispered.

He tipped his head back, locking his gaze with mine as he slowly slid a finger inside me. "The ridges of a Taori horn are as sensitive during the Quaibyn as..." His thumb found my clit, and he pressed it. "What do you call this?"

Flames licked at my cheeks. "A clit."

He circled his thumb, and I moaned. As if driven by instinct to hear more of my hungry cries, he returned his mouth to my clit, swirling his tongue and dragging his finger in and out so mercilessly that I was panting and biting down on my bottom lip to keep from screaming. As my body started to spasm, I stroked the ridges of his horns harder, and his rumbling growls vibrated his lips.

"Fuck yes," I gritted out, as waves of pleasure ricocheted through me, hot and fierce, and I held his face to me by the horns. When I stopped spasming and my grip on his horns dropped, Torst stood swiftly, dragging his cock through my slickness.

His gaze locked on mine as he thrust inside me in a single fast movement, and I opened my mouth in shock, even though no sound emerged. I would have been stretched by a cock as thick as his anyway, but one with three heads down the length of it was like being entered three times, each crown stretching me a bit more than the last. When I'd taken the last crown to the hilt, I arched my body into him.

I was still spasming from the orgasm he'd given me with his tongue and taking him so deep sent even more pulses of pleasure through me—now mixed with a flash of pain as my body adjusted to him. I clenched around his cock, my fingers slipping down his shoulders and scoring his chest muscles with my nails.

"So tight," he husked as he held himself deep.

Torst's skin burned, sweat beading as his muscles bunched with tension. He needed more than being inside me—and so did I.

"I won't break if you fuck me hard," I whispered, liking the sound of the forbidden words on my lips almost as much as I liked being taken up against the stone wall.

"You want it hard, don't you?"

I moaned, unwilling to admit what I wanted even though my body ached for him to move inside me.

"You want to see if you're tough enough to handle being fucked by an alien like me, don't you, little female?"

"I'm not a little—" I started to say, but he cut off my words with a thick hand clamped over my mouth.

"You're my little female, and you're going to take everything I give you, aren't you?" He drove himself deeper in me, all gentleness gone from him as he panted in my ear. "Aren't you?"

I nodded with a smothered cry as he held his hand tight across my mouth.

"That's my good, little female. Taking my cock like you were born to fuck me." His words were hot and slurred as he bit the lobe of my ear and thrust so hard my feet lifted from the ground. "Maybe you were born to fuck me. Maybe you were put on this moon so I could find you and fuck you. What do you think, female? Was your body made to take my cock deep like this?"

My head swam as unwanted desire jack-knifed through me. Whatever resistance he'd felt was gone as he rutted into me hard and fast. Only the arm bracing my back and hand curled around my head kept me from getting dragged up and down the stone wall. I tried to move but his grasp on me was complete. I couldn't resist, and I couldn't stop myself from moaning and opening my legs wider for him.

He was right. My body reacted as if this was what I'd been waiting for, his dominant claiming firing something deep within me. I wanted to take everything he could give me. I *needed* to.

"You're mine, Lia." He nipped the tender flesh of my neck. "You can try to run, but I'll always find you, little one. Find you and fuck you the way you like it."

My pleasure-drugged brain was addled by his shift from protector to possessor, even as his coarse words made my nipples pebble with arousal.

He slipped his hand from my mouth to my neck, tilting my head up and feathering his lips over mine. "You do like being fucked hard, don't you?"

I moaned my yes and lifted my leg higher around his waist, unable to form coherent words as his three crowns thrust in me again and again, the stretching sensation intense.

He tightened his grip on my neck. "Tell me. I want to hear you say it."

Even with his hand curled around my neck, his cock splitting me, and his tail wrapped around my leg, I met his gaze with my own defiant one. "You first."

He growled, closed his eyes, and dragged his tail up my bare leg. "If you keep taking my cock like you were made for it, you might drive me mad before the fever does or before we lock."

I jerked from my haze. "Lock?"

He stroked his cock in and out. "With the fever comes the mating clench." He grunted. "I'll be locked inside your sweet, tight sex until it passes."

Mating clench? If I hadn't been so breathless and dazed, I might have panicked, but my brain was too clouded by my desire and by how well he was filling me. At this point, I didn't care if his cock was buried in me forever.

"As long as you don't stop," I whispered.

Torst scooped my ass in his hands and lifted me up with his cock still buried inside me, walking me to the grass-filled mattress and lowering us both until I was on my back and his body was braced above me.

"I couldn't stop if I wanted to—or if you wanted me to." He leaned back and spread my legs wide, looking down as his eyes sparked with carnal desire. "Sons of the goddess, you're perfect."

Then he fell forward and smothered my gasps with his mouth, as he started to fuck me hard and fast.

I wrapped my legs around his waist, my hips instinctively thrusting up to match his movements as his tongue tangled with mine. Each of his cockheads rubbed a different part of me as he drove in and out, the delicious friction making my body tremble with another fast release. My cries were swallowed by his mouth as I came again, but Torst didn't slow his punishing pace.

My legs trembled as I held onto his slippery back, but just as quickly as he'd flopped me onto the mattress, he flipped me over and pulled me onto my hands and knees, whispering into my ear as he grasped a handful of my hair, "Just in case you think you can escape from me."

Then he tilted my ass into the air and drove into me from behind. I bit down on my lip until I tasted blood, throwing my head back. If I'd thought he'd been deep before, this new angle was even deeper. Instinctively, I tried to move away, but he jerked my body back.

Leaning over me, his hot body cocooned mine. "You think you can get away before I'm done claiming you, little female?"

I twitched my ass, but he'd impaled me so thoroughly my body barely moved. I craned my head to look back at him, inhaling a shocked breath when I saw his inked chest glistening with sweat and his horns lowered as he powered into me. His tail swished behind him, making him look even more like an alien beast driven by mating fever. A hint of fear teased the base of my spine, but it was quickly doused when the furry tip of his tail slid between my legs and stroked my clit.

A moan escaped my lips as he tugged on my hair and thrust deep, his tail quivering over my clit. My legs were already weak when he clasped my hips and pistoned into me with a renewed ferocity, giving a final hard thrust and pulsing hot and fast. But before he was even done, Torst had twisted me, so I was facing him again, his cock still lodged inside me as he collapsed onto the mattress and pulled me on top of him.

I sagged onto his chest, releasing a contented sigh before jerking up when I felt his cock swelling inside me. "Did your cock just get bigger?"

Then the words "mating clench" resurfaced in my mind.

He rolled me over onto my back, resting his forehead on mine as his breath came out in uneven gasps. "When I said you could not escape from me, I meant it, Lia."

CHAPTER
TWENTY-EIGHT

Torst

My body no longer trembled, the feverish heat already cooling as the madness faded. Now that I'd claimed her, the pounding need that had ravaged my body was gone, but the swelling of the three knobs of my cock locked me to her. They would unlock one at a time, starting with the top, until the last crown locked at the base where our bodies met finally resumed its normal size, but not until we'd been forced together long enough to secure the mating and douse the fever entirely.

She wasn't the first female I'd been locked with, but she was the first human. My gaze quickly scanned her face for signs that I'd hurt her.

"Was I too rough?" I asked, raising a hand to her hair and brushing aside a damp strand.

Her eyes were wide as she stared up at me, shaking her

head. "No. I'm fine." Then her gaze darted down. "This is the mating clench?"

"Each crown swells and then releases. The one at the base releases last, which is why it feels so tight." I leaned more on one elbow so as not to crush her and attempted to pull away slightly, but the lock between our bodies was so snug she gasped. I stilled, moving myself closer again.

The wrinkle between her brows relaxed. "I like the feel of you inside me. Human men can't do this."

I studied her face, loving the glow that I'd given her skin and the "just-been-fucked" flare of her pupils. "No? What do human males do after mating?"

She snorted out a laugh then covered her mouth and giggled more softly. "Usually, they roll over and start snoring."

I frowned at this. That didn't sound very pleasurable. "I promise I will not start snoring."

Her gaze slid to the side. "Snoring wouldn't be louder than what we just did. I'm sure everyone in the tunnels heard."

A strange possessive thrill filled me. "I do not mind if they know I claimed you. Do you have a problem with them knowing you are mine?"

"When you say that I'm yours...?"

"I have just claimed you during the Quaibyn fever, and we are joined in the fever clench. I felt you come on my tongue and my cock. Do you doubt that you are mine, little one?"

She frowned. "I'm not little."

I thrilled at the sight of her ire and the flash of her eyes, loving even more that she couldn't run from me. "To me, you are small, mate."

"Mate?" She drew in a quick breath. "I thought you just needed a willing female to burn off the fever."

I flinched at this. "You are not just any female." My gaze

drifted from her eyes which were still half-lidded with sated desire to the curve of her lips, and my heart squeezed. It had been so long since I'd felt anything when I'd been with a female and not since Kaolin that I'd felt this content. I couldn't explain how I could feel pulled to a creature who was so different and who came from a planet so far away from my home world, but as I held her with my gaze, I could almost feel the bonds knitting between us.

Sons of the goddess, this was more than the mating fever and clench, I thought. My gaze pinned her as I struggled to breathe, overwhelmed with the sense that I'd known Lia for so much longer than a few paltry astro-days. As impossible as it was, she felt as familiar to me as any of my Taori brothers. Her brown eyes pulled me in so fully it was like I was drowning in her—but the contentment that filled my soul made me welcome going under so deep I had to remember how to breathe.

"What are you doing?"

I blinked at her question as she jerked her gaze from mine. "What do you mean?"

"That thing with your eyes. Were you putting me under a spell?"

The heat from her body pulsed into mine, and her heart felt like it was beating in my chest. Had I been entrancing her with my gaze? "There is no spell. But one of the Taori love litanies says, 'I am bound by your eyes and to your heart.' We believe the eyes are the key to melding souls."

I'd often used my gaze to hold the attention of other creatures. It had never been a conscious effort to entrance them, but like all Taori, I knew the power of the gaze to mirror the heart and soul. The eyes were as much a part of the mating clench bonding as the swell of the cock—or the whispering of words.

"As I blanket your body with mine, I require as many kisses

as there are stars in the sky," I said, kissing my across her jawline to her ear and nibbling it.

Our people were guided by our ancient wisdom and words, and I'd learned not to doubt the power of either. If they could guide us in battle, they could guide our souls. Our people had always believed in souls being led to each other. Why not across space and time? If Lia was fated to be mine, not even centuries and galaxies could stand in the way.

She returned her eyes to mine, "So, now you're back to being a sweet-talker?"

"You did not think my talking earlier was sweet? Did you not like it?"

She shot me what she must have intended to be a severe look but ended up as a stifled smirk. "I didn't say I didn't like it."

My lips hovered over hers, brushing her soft skin with a gentle kiss. "Good."

She huffed out a warm breath that mingled with mine. "You know, you aren't like any other guy I've ever been with."

I tilted my head at her, not sure of her meaning. "Is that good?"

"It's good but it's a lot to get used to. Most human men don't talk about being bound, and..." She drew her bottom lip up and nibbled it. "I've never heard of a cock with three..."

"Crowns?" I finished for her. "I understand it isn't common, but I admit that I don't know much about other species' anatomy, unless they are female."

She gave me a scandalized look. "How many other species' females?"

I smiled at her, running a finger down one cheek. "It doesn't matter now. I cannot imagine a species I could prefer more than humans."

She cocked one eyebrow. "Does this mean you have a desire to sample more human women?"

I frowned at this, even though I knew she was serious. "Why would I need to try another human when you're so perfect?" I released a low rumble in my chest as I shifted inside her. "I can't imagine another human taking me as well as you did."

She blinked rapidly, her pupils flaring.

"Does it bother you?" I asked, curious by this reaction. "Do you not like to talk about how well you took my cock?"

Her chest heaved. "No, I like it but it's hard to hear you talk like that and not want to..."

A rumble rose in my core. "You wish me to fuck you again, don't you?"

She slapped my chest gently. "Shh. The others will hear you. I'm sure we already woke them."

I bent my head so that my lips were at her ear. "Believe me, I would love nothing more than to feel your body writhing beneath mine, but the fever clench makes it impossible for us to separate or for me to move."

She gave a small shake of her head. "It's okay. It feels... good." Her gaze darted down. "Tight and full. It's like my body was waiting to be filled by you."

My heart constricted at this, even as her eyes watered. It made no sense to feel the same inevitability, but I did. The lust that had first been triggered by the Quaibyn had quickly morphed into more as I'd seen glimpses of her heart and her inner strength. Now, it seemed like I was always meant to be pulled through time and space so I could be in this very space with Lia as the clench melted the pain that had been clutching my heart for so long.

"I'm sorry." The words rushed from her mouth. "That was a cheesy thing to say."

I dragged the pad of my thumb across her plump bottom lip. "I do not know what that would have to do with cheese, but do not apologize. I have never experienced such a perfect melding of bodies before." I hesitated, my voice gruff. "Not even with my Taori intended."

She stopped breathing as she gazed up at me, finally swallowing hard. "You were engaged?"

It should have felt odd to be discussing a past love while my cock was locked inside her, but the intense bonding sensation made it possible for me to think about the past without the usual ache.

"Her name was Kaolin, and we were intended to be joined together in the Taori bonding ceremony." Usually, thinking of Kaolin filled me with pain and rage, but not now.

"What happened?" Lia asked softly.

"She was killed in the initial Sythian attack. They're the mutant beasts my people are chasing across the galaxy." I paused, thinking about the hundreds of years that had passed when we'd been sucked through the temporal wormhole. "At least, we were. I don't know what happened to the scourge or to my brothers in pursuit."

"I'm sorry, Torst."

I met her gaze and saw my own pain reflected in her eyes. I released a breath and brushed my lips across hers. "It was long ago."

"Time doesn't take away pain. It can only dull the sting."

I nuzzled her neck and breathed in the comforting scent of her skin. "You're wise for one so young."

She giggled as I nipped at the tender skin of her throat. "Young? How old are you?"

"Many decades older than you, I suspect."

"Decades? You don't look decades older than me. You can't be older than thirty-five, forty, tops."

I pulled back, grinning and shifting my weight as the grass crackled under us. "Taori live at least twice as long as humans, that I do know. My crew has been journeying across the galaxies for longer than you've been alive."

Her eyebrows shot up. "Really? Then I'm even more impressed with your staying power, old man."

"Old man?" A deep chuckle escaped from my lips, and I tilted my hips back so that my cock moved even deeper inside her.

Her dark pupils flared, and her mouth formed a perfect O. "That's not fair."

I slid an arm underneath her body and pulled her flush to me. "What isn't fair is how much I want to fuck you again, and this time I don't care if we make the rocks tremble from our screams."

"Torst!"

What was even more unfair—and what I couldn't tell her yet—was how claiming her had filled me with an even more fiercely overwhelming need to protect her. Now that I'd found such a perfect mate—one who had quenched my mating fever as if she'd been born for it—I couldn't lose her.

No matter what.

CHAPTER
TWENTY-NINE

Lia

The echoing voices were what first woke me, then I lifted my head from Torst's chest. We were still in the alcove and the curtain hung over the opening, but the others were clearly awake and moving about the tunnels.

My face heated at the thought that they'd all heard us the night before. No way had anyone slept through all that growling and flesh slapping flesh. The warmth spread from my cheeks to my core, and finally heat throbbed between my legs at the loud memories.

At some point, Torst's cock had released me from its lock—or the mating clench, as he'd called it—and he'd reluctantly pulled from me. After being filled so snugly by him for so long, I'd almost immediately longed for him again, but I'd also craved sleep. My body had been overcome by exhaustion—a combination of the stress of the past few days and the frenzied exertion of Torst's mating fever—and I'd curled up next to him and drifted off to sleep.

Even though I'd been sleeping next to an alien I'd only just met, my rest had been deep and untroubled by nightmares, which was unusual. My sleep was typically fitful and marred by dark dreams I rarely remembered. But not last night. Burning off Torst's mating fever had also done something to me. I tried not to think about his talk of bonding or how his penetrating gaze had made me feel a connection to him that was surprisingly deep.

Torst shifted as he lifted his arms and folded them behind his head, peering down at me. "You're awake."

I shouldn't have felt shy—after all, I'd been locked in a mating clench by his cock—but I wasn't sure what had changed between us. The deal I'd made with myself was that I'd help him cure his mating fever. I'd never considered anything more, even though it was hard to think that things hadn't changed. You couldn't be locked body-to-body with someone without forming a deeper connection, and hearing Torst talk about his former fiancée and his painful past had softened my heart to him.

"I'm awake." I pushed myself up, propping on one arm to look at him more fully. There was enough light from the common area to cast a glow across his tattooed chest and make his silver horns shimmer within his dark hair. My breath caught in my throat as I thought back to holding onto those horns while his head had been buried between my legs, and my pussy twitched in response, which made me flinch slightly.

His brow furrowed. "You're in pain?"

"I'm a little sore is all." Not that shocking since I'd had an enormous cock with three crowns lodged inside me.

He cupped my face in one of his large hands. "I should have tried to control my fever."

"Is that possible?"

"The Quaibyn affects everyone a bit differently. Some Taori lose all sense of themselves and have little memory of burning off their fever, but I'm one of the lucky ones." He sat up, his stomach muscles rippling. "I remember every moment of being inside you." He pulled my face to his, kissing me gently. "And of tasting you."

I stole a glance at the opening in the curtain, and Torst laughed.

"You're worried they will hear me talking of the mating they all heard last night?"

I shot him a look. "We do have to leave this area at some point, and I'd like to be able to look the other survivors in the eyes."

He kissed me again, and this kiss was deeper and more claiming. "Why would you not? Do humans feel shame after mating?"

I let out a breath. How was I supposed to explain human morality and my mother's obsession that I not be corrupted by bad boys to a Taori who came from a world where mating fever —and female priestesses to tend to it—were as normal as breathing?

"Not always, but we usually try not to be so loud about it."

He tilted his head at me and grinned. "That was not loud, Lia. I didn't even let out the mating scream."

The mating scream? "Is that something I have to look forward to?"

He pulled me to him, and something hard bumped my stomach. "You might not have to wait long."

Pushing him away and jumping up, I scanned the stone floor for my pants and panties. "Oh, no. Not with everyone awake and just outside the curtain. I may not be a prude, but I'm also not going to put on a free show." I found my panties and yanked them on inside out, wishing I had a clean change of clothes. "Besides, aren't we supposed to go over our plan of attack?"

Torst huffed out a disappointed sigh, standing up and stretching, even though his arms couldn't extend over his head, considering the low ceiling. He made no move to cover himself, or rush to put on pants, and my gaze was drawn to the cock hanging between his legs. Even when it wasn't rigid and engorged, it was impressive. Part of me still didn't know how I'd managed to take all of it, although I felt the ache now.

I pulled on my pants, snatching his up from the floor and handing them to him. "You'd better get dressed unless you want to give our new friends the shock of their lives."

I didn't add how lucky we were that none of them had walked out when he was completely naked and in the grip of the fever the night before. At least there was no reason to have to explain the Taori mating fever to them and have them worry that Torst might be a threat. We needed all the allies we could get if we were going to take on the Xulonians and escape from their hunting moon.

I smoothed my torn shirt and swept my hair back up into a ponytail, turning and preparing myself to join the others. Before I could pull back the curtain, Torst caught my arm and spun me around and into his arms.

I braced my hands on his bare chest, the hard muscles now familiar to me. "What happened to focusing on the mission?"

He put a finger under my chin and tipped my face to his. "I wouldn't be able to focus on the mission if it wasn't for you. I'd still be gripped with the fever and possibly running mad through the tunnels, or on the surface of the moon."

I wasn't sure how to respond to him basically thanking me for fucking the fever from him. "I couldn't let that happen. Not after you saved my life."

He nodded, his penetrating blue eyes locked on mine and reminding me of how deeply connected we'd been. Each time he pinned me with his gaze, I felt an unmistakable pull toward him, as if I was sinking deeper and deeper into a euphoric quicksand. He might claim his eyes didn't have a special power, but their intensity made me feel almost lightheaded, and there was no denying that my connection to him grew with every glance.

"Now we've saved each other—and we belong to each other," he said. "You do know that last night was only the beginning of us, don't you?"

I sucked in a quick breath. I'd thought his talk of claiming and of me being his had been because he'd been in the throes of the fever, but maybe not. Instead of this freaking me out—I *had* just met the alien—I was filled with a sense of contentment. It might be a bit crazy and impulsive, but it felt right. He felt right.

I slid my hands from his chest up into his hair until I'd gripped his horns. The whites of his eyes flashed desire, and he growled.

I tugged his head down until our eyes were level, letting out a growl of my own. "Bring it on, sweet talker."

CHAPTER
THIRTY

Torst

I took the bowl that was offered to me, crouching down on my haunches instead of perching on one of the low log seats gathered around the fire.

"The Xulonians eat a sweet porridge for breakfast," Zennen said, passing an identical bowl to Lia and returning to his seat. "It's an acquired taste."

After a night of energetic mating, my stomach rumbled in anticipation. I cut my gaze to Lia, who'd already taken a bite and was chewing it slowly as her eyelashes fluttered rapidly.

She swallowed and took a swig from a water pouch. "Very sweet."

I took a hesitant bite, prodded by my hunger. She was right. The goopy, blue substance was a strange mix of pungent and painfully sweet. I swallowed it, taking another spoonful. At least it was filling my empty belly. I'd need sustenance if I was going to mount an attack on our enemy.

162

"Sleep well?" Rafe asked, as he joined the group, running a hand through his hair and grinning.

It was obvious this question was meant for me and Lia, and even more obvious that he was enjoying the way she squirmed.

"I slept well." I leveled my gaze at him. "I always sleep well after I bed a beautiful female." Lia's mouth gaped open, and she swung her head in my direction, but I didn't look away from the alien firestarter. "Does it bother you to hear the sounds of mating?"

He shrugged. "I guess we don't have to wonder if you two are together anymore."

"You don't." My voice was low and held a warning in it. "Lia is my mine."

Lia cleared her throat. "If the pissing contest portion of breakfast is over, are we going to talk about the attack plan?"

Rafe laughed, rubbing his hands together and sending up sparks. "Just tell me what to set on fire and when."

Zennen held up his palms. "I don't think we want to burn anything."

I eyed Rafe, whose eyes danced with mischief. He was no more than a youngling who enjoyed testing limits. Now that I'd established that Lia was mine, I had no problem with the alien, and his ability to start fires would be useful.

"On the contrary." I scooped the last bit of porridge from my bowl and wiped my mouth with the back of my hand, "I want to burn this moon to ash."

Rafe made a fist with one hand and pumped it toward his body. "Yes!"

Zennen stammered out a series of unintelligible words, his antennae bobbling, before finally saying, "But we'll all be burned along with it."

"Not if we leave," I said. "I have no intention of remaining one of these Xulonians' prisoners or prey. If there are ships that bring the director and his staff to the moon, then there's a way for us to escape."

Zennen leaned forward, his own bowl of food forgotten. "And go where? The Xulonian planetary defenses are advanced."

"But I doubt they'd blow their own ships from the air."

Lia smiled at me. "If we jam communications first, then the aliens on the home world won't know about the attack here, or that the ship leaving the surface is filled with survivors of their hunt."

I inclined my head at her. I loved that she wasn't some delicate female who knew nothing of warfare and defense. Despite her size—and my initial misgivings about her strength—Lia clearly understood military strategy. "Our first goal should be to disable their communications systems." I slid my gaze to Baboo. "You created these tunnels. You must know the most about their buildings, since your tunnels extend into them."

"Not all of them." The alien rubbed a hand nervously over the brown spikes on his head. "I don't have a tunnel that leads into the main command center, but the supply storage building is not far from it."

"Do the Xulonians run communications from the command center?" Lia asked.

"They must," Baboo said. "There is no other building where we've seen the aliens, aside from the avatars who roam around hunting."

"Do the avatars look like the Xulonians?" Lia shuddered, as she no doubt recalled the red-skinned creatures who'd nearly killed her.

Zennen nodded, his shared distaste obvious in his expression. "The red skulls appear as they are."

"I guess they like being ugly pricks," Lia said.

"Then we need to breech the command center to take out

communications." I put my bowl down on the floor and clasped my hands together as I thought. "Do we have any idea how much security they have on the building?"

Rafe choked back a laugh. "They don't need much. Who's going to attack them? All the prey they get from slavers are unarmed and don't last long on the surface. From what we can tell, either they don't match up the kills with the prey, or they don't care that there are some of us who were never killed."

"They might have assumed we were taken by the sea." Yara flipped her white hair off her shoulder. "Or sucked under in the bogs."

Lia blinked at her. "There are bogs?"

"There is much of this moon you've yet to see," Yara told her.

As unpleasant as the bogs sounded, I was encouraged that the Xulonians were so confident in their dominion over the hunting moon. They'd underestimated the aliens they'd brought to hunt without mercy, and they would pay dearly for their hubris.

"The most dangerous time to be near the command center is when a new crop of hunters is released," Zennen said.

"When does that happen?" I asked.

He drummed his thin fingers together. "Not at any set time but always in the daytime."

"And always after a shipment of slaves." Rafe's mischievous expression darkened and wiped away his air of youthfulness. "They like to hunt during the day. Better odds."

I let out a derisive grunt. "I'll take my odds against their version of hunters, but if we can avoid their hunting party, it will draw less attention."

"If you need a distraction," Rafe held out a palm as a ball of flames danced within it, "just say the word."

I thought about how I wanted to go into the command

center. I wasn't against a hard and brutal incursion, but that increased the chances of them tipping off the home planet. That was a risk not worth taking.

"Let's wait until we've secured our ship to scorch our enemy."

Rafe twitched one shoulder. "I can wait."

"When do we track down Val?"

I turned to Lia. Her missing friend and shipmate had slipped my mind. I'd been so distracted by stumbling onto the other survivors and dousing my mating fever with a night of glorious mating that I'd forgotten about finding the other human and any more Taori who might have crashed onto the moon as well.

"We can't burn this place to the ground before we find her," Lia insisted, her expression just as stubborn as ever.

"Who is Val?" Zennen cocked his head in interest.

"Another human who was brought to the planet with Lia," I said. "She was injured as they ran from the hunters and then disappeared from their hiding spot."

The faces around the fire were grim as no one spoke.

"I know what you're thinking." Lia shook her head and her long tail of hair swung from side to side. "But she's not dead. We saw no evidence she was killed or taken from the cave against her will."

Baboo jerked up, the tips of his brown spikes reddening. "Did you say she was hiding in a cave?"

I almost groaned out loud. Of course. "Are you saying that cave might be connected to these underground tunnels?"

Lia looked at me, her brows pressed together. "We were in that cave. I didn't see any entrance to a tunnel."

"Some of them are hidden behind twists or bends. You might not have noticed it if you weren't looking," Baboo said as his leg jiggled.

"But why would she have gone into a tunnel if she knew I was coming back?" Lia asked. "And why wouldn't she have shown herself when I returned. Torst and I were there for a while waiting for the mercenaries to pass."

"That I can't tell you, but it would explain some of the noises we heard before you arrived."

My pulse quickened. "What noises?"

Rafe's wicked grin was back in full force as he looked at me. "Growls like the ones that kept me up last night."

THIRTY-ONE

Lia

All eyes swung to Torst, including mine.

"It must be one of my kinsmen." He stood and paced behind the circle of makeshift seats ringing the glowing ball of fire. "Most of us were able to get out in escape pods. More than only mine did land on this moon."

I turned and followed his brisk pace with my gaze, wondering why he seemed so agitated at this news. "You were hoping to find another Taori on the surface. Isn't it good news that one might have found the tunnel system? At least that's evidence they haven't been captured by the hunters or mercenaries."

Torst laughed roughly. "As if one of the Xulonian hunters could take down a Taori."

I gave his cockiness a pass since he *had* eliminated every member of the alien hunters chasing me. "Okay, it's a good sign the mercenaries haven't gotten to him."

Torst grunted, and I wasn't sure if it was a sound of agreement or disagreement. Finally, he stopped pacing, whirling to face the group. "This changes the plan. First we need to search for Val and my fellow Taori."

I agreed with his assessment. I wasn't going to be a part of burning down the hunting moon—literally—with one of the shipmates I'd sworn to protect on it. But I was curious by how adamant he was, and how discovering that Baboo and Rafe had heard Taori sounds had upset him. I didn't feel like this was the kind of conversation I wanted to have in front of the other survivors, though.

"Can we start a search of the tunnels?" I pivoted back to Baboo. "If you heard noises not long ago, chances are good whomever made them is still down here."

The other survivors exchanged nervous glances.

Zennen broke the uncomfortable silence. "The tunnels are a bit of a labyrinth. I would not wish you to wander them without a guide who knows them well."

"That isn't all of you?" I peered from face to face as heads shook and gazes darted to the floor.

Baboo puffed out his chest. "I know them because I made most of them."

"And I know them because I can't stand to stay under here for too long." Rafe shifted the orb of fire from one open palm to the other like a hot potato.

"How long will it take to make a complete search?" Torst asked.

"One team going up and back every tunnel?" Baboo peered up at the ceiling, as if he'd find the answer written there. "Maybe a single standard rotation? Maybe two if we take breaks to rest and eat."

Torst scowled. "That long?"

"They do run beneath the entire moon, which isn't a small as you might think," Zennen said.

"We don't have that kind of time," Torst snapped, his sharp words reverberating around us and making everyone jump. He seemed to realize how loud he'd spoken, and he steadied his voice. "I don't mean to raise my voice, but if the other human is still alive, we need to find her fast—before the hunters or mercenaries do."

This was true, but I had a sinking feeling this wasn't why Torst was so determined to make the search as fast as possible.

"Why don't we split up into teams?" I suggested. "If both Rafe and Baboo know the tunnels, we can each go with one of them."

Before Rafe could speak, Torst pinned him with an intimidating look. "I will go with Rafe."

The pale-haired alien grinned at him, amused he'd been claimed so quickly and in no doubt as to why. "I'm flattered."

Torst growled as the alien continued to grin merrily at him.

I stood and walked over to Torst, tugging his arm as I passed and pulling him back into the alcove we'd shared. "What was that?"

He tilted his head as he peered down at me. "What?"

I folded my arms across my chest and lowered my voice to a whisper. "You picked Rafe so I'd be with Baboo."

"You don't like Baboo?"

I rolled my eyes. "I like Baboo just fine, but why don't you trust me with Rafe?"

"It isn't you I don't trust." He cast a glance and a growl at the curtain behind which the firestarter alien sat.

"He's harmless," I said, "and he's just a kid."

"He looks like a kid." Torst wagged a finger at me. "We have no idea his true age."

"It doesn't matter. I'm not interested in him." I glared at the

Taori. "Do you really think I would spend the night with you inside me and then start something up with Rafe?"

He shifted, shaking his head brusquely.

"Good, because I'm not that kind of girl." I didn't say that I was also not the kind of girl who usually ended up in a mating fever clench with an alien she barely knew.

He closed the slight distance between us, slipping an arm around my waist and tugging me so that my body brushed his. "The Taori can be possessive about their mates. I won't apologize for that, little female."

I decided to let it slide because if I was being honest, hearing him call me his mate sent a thrill of pleasure through me—almost as much as being called his little female triggered a throb of desire. I put a hand to his chest, more to steady myself than to keep him at bay. "What was all that about finding Val as fast as possible? What's really going on?"

He cut his gaze to the opening in the curtain. "It isn't your friend we need to find so quickly, although I also wish to save her. It's my Taori brother who needs to be tracked down."

His choice of words gave me pause. "Why?"

"If Rafe heard the same sounds I made while in my mating frenzy with you then that means that my Taori brother is also afflicted with the fever."

I thought of the pretty scientist with her wounded ankle. "You don't think...?"

A scowl was etched onto his face. "A Taori male would never intentionally harm or force himself on a female, but the mating fever affects each male differently, and we are not ourselves when we're in the clutches of the fever."

My gut tightened. That meant Valeria might be in more than one type of imminent danger.

THIRTY-TWO

Torst

"It's not bad in the tunnels with the right light." Rafe walked ahead of me, a spinning ball of flames hovering over his open palm.

I didn't answer because his statement didn't require an answer, although he twisted his head back and caught my eye, as if he expected something from me. I grunted, and the throaty sound echoed back.

The alien turned back so he faced ahead, the light in his hand sending shadows bouncing across the rock ceiling and walls and extending a gold glow several metrons ahead of us. He was right. This was much preferable to walking through the maze of tunnels in the dark, although I didn't require the light, and I would have preferred the company of Lia.

"You're probably wondering how I came to be here on this moon," Rafe continued, his other arm swinging by his side. "And why I didn't burn it all down before now."

I glanced at the male's scruffy pale hair from behind. I hadn't wondered that before, but now I did.

"I wasn't dropped in the jungle or forest to be hunted," Rafe said without waiting for my response. "Those cold-blooded Xulonians put me on frozen tundra."

"Ice?" That would make his fire-starting powers less potent.

"And snow. Lots of it." The flame in his hand flared larger and brighter. "My attempts to start fires just made water. I almost drowned myself."

"How many of your kind were brought here?" I asked.

Rafe shrugged. "Not many. I guess they thought since Berrians aren't huge and covered in armor or scales, we were good prey. But even though I couldn't start much of a blaze, I could set their avatars on fire." He chuckled. "They didn't like that."

"Berrians?"

He jerked a thumb at his chest with his free hand. "That's what I am. From the planet Berea." He stole another quick glance at me. "Ever heard of us?"

"No, but I'm not from this galaxy."

Rafe stumbled and the fire flickered. "Then how did you end up here?"

"A temporal wormhole."

"That explains it," the fire starter mumbled, more to himself than to me.

I wondered what he meant, but I didn't want to ask him and encourage his chatter. He hadn't stopped talking since we'd started down the tunnel, and I was regretting picking him as a search partner. Baboo had seemed quiet, and I doubted he was pestering Lia with constant chatter. Then I recalled how Rafe had looked at Lia and why I'd insisted on pairing off with him.

Despite Lia's protests, I had no issue trusting her, and I didn't believe she would be lured in by the alien's quick-talking charm. But knowing that he would be looking at her like she was a meal made me want to slam him against a wall—and then press Lia up against a wall and claim her in front of him so he would have no doubt that the pretty human was mine.

"You okay?"

I jerked up to find Rafe glancing back at me with his brows raised. "I am fine. Why do you ask?"

"You were growling—more than usual."

I grunted. "I was thinking about the Xulonians and how I look forward to making them pay for their cruelty."

He nodded. "They're bad ones. Not that they always were."

"No? I've found that souls are not eaten away and replaced by darkness overnight."

He whistled. "That's deep. I guess you're right, but it did take a while for the Xulonians to become what they are today. Generations of isolation and seeing any other species as so far beneath them that they are expendable turned them into monsters."

"The other planets don't come after them for gross violations of interplanetary treaties?"

Rafe emitted a dark laugh, and his flame dimmed. "This galaxy has no such treaties. Any peace was shattered millennia ago. The empire saw to that."

It was hard for me to imagine a future where planets didn't have treaties. I'd just come from forming a partnership with the Drexians to fight the Sythian swarm together. Into what kind of future had I been thrust?

"The empire?"

Rafe nodded. "Your girl works for them. Their insignia is on her shirt."

I'd noticed an insignia on Lia's chest but hadn't thought to ask what it meant. I'd been too busy saving her and then claiming her.

"The empire doesn't protect planets from Xulonians?"

Rafe shot me a look of pity over his shoulder. "Not unless there's profit in it for them. I'm sure they'll be upset they lost your girl and whoever else was with her when her imperial ship was taken, but they don't dare attack the Xulonians. Not when so many slavers and pirates help protect Xulonian space."

My stomach tightened. Lia worked for an empire that would allow slavery and murder? I shook my head at the thought. That didn't make sense. Not when I'd seen how honorable she was and how valiantly she'd insisted on finding her shipmate. Then my throat went dry. Unless she was only bent on saving her shipmate because Val was an asset to the empire.

Dark thoughts swirled through my mind as I went over everything Lia had told me about Val and about her ship. Had she been lying to me or was she unaware of her empire's craven attitudes?

"I'm guessing the empire isn't in charge in your time or in your galaxy?"

Rafe's question brought me back to the present, and I focused on the seemingly endless tunnel we trudged down. "No. There is no empire that rules my galaxy, and the only empire we've encountered recently is the Drexian Empire, and they would never allow this."

"Drexians." Rafe said the word slowly. "I've heard of them, but their reach has never extended to here. Neither has the Taori, although I've heard tales of your journey."

Now I almost stumbled, righting myself with a hand on the wall, the porous rock scraping my flesh. "You have heard of my people?"

He shrugged. "Not recently."

I narrowed my gaze at his back as he walked ahead of me, curiosity pricking the back of my neck. "Tell me, Rafe. How old are you?"

He laughed. "I wondered when you'd ask. You're quiet, but clever."

I didn't speak, and silence filled the tunnel for the first time since we'd left the gathering place where the other survivors remained.

"My kind don't measure time in the same way as most, but I would be several hundred of the standard astro-years."

I let this sink in. I'd suspected he was older than he appeared and that his shaggy appearance was a ruse to seem younger, but I hadn't expected him to have lived for so long already. "We might have shared history after all."

Rafe gave me a disarming grin that almost made me forget he was my elder—by a lot. "Like I said, I know of your journey and of the swarm you chased."

The knot that had formed in my gut tightened. "You know of the Sythian swarm? Does that mean you know if we were victorious in defeating them and saving the galaxies in their path?"

He hesitated, his boyish grin faltering and giving rise to a sick feeling that he was avoiding sharing bad news with me. No pronouncement of victory was ever preceded by a painful pause. I almost didn't want to hear it, the idea of knowing the fate of my Taori brothers, whose bones were already ash in the wind, sent a cold shiver down my spine.

Before I could stop him from revealing the fate of Taori and our foe, a scream pierced the air. A female's scream.

All fear for my dead kinsman was forgotten as I spun toward the sound. "Lia."

Then Rafe and I both started running.

THIRTY-THREE

Lia

The sound of our footfall on the stone was a steady patter as Baboo and I walked side by side through the tunnels. One of Rafe's self-contained orbs of fire levitated in front of us, held in place by Baboo's telekinetic powers. We'd been walking in silence since we'd split from Torst and Rafe. They'd gone down one fork in the tunnels, and Baboo had chosen the other side.

"I'm guessing this is one of the tunnels you created?" I said, breaking the silence.

He snuck a bashful glance at me. "It is." He nodded his spiky head at the walls. "You can tell because my tunneling is smoother than anything nature created."

I gave an appreciative nod, even though I doubted I could tell a big difference between types of rock walls. "It's crazy that the Xulonians don't know about the tunnels. I get that they don't know about the new ones you made, but you'd think they'd be aware of the preexisting, natural ones. It is their moon, after all."

"A moon they never visited until they needed it to entertain their citizens who wanted to escape the dark reality of a destroyed planet without actually leaving it."

"Their planet is destroyed?"

Baboo frowned and nodded. "I only know because once my species conducted trade with the Xulonians."

"You had diplomatic relations with them, and they ended up taking you as a slave to be hunted?"

"Our relationship with them was over long before I was taken, but I know the stories. They've always been xenophobic, but there was a time they would conduct trade for things they could not produce themselves. As their fear of other species increased, they cut off trade and relied more on their own planet's resources as their population grew. They mined it mercilessly until nothing was left."

"Let me guess how that turned out." I didn't bother keeping the snark from my voice.

Baboo cut his gaze to me. "Not well for their environment as you well guessed. From all reports, Xulon is overpopulated and polluted."

"Yet they still refuse to leave?"

"Fear is the most powerful emotion. It causes creatures to kill and be killed."

I shook my head, my gaze trained on the glow lighting our way down the pitch-black path. How had I not heard of Xulon's crimes, and why wasn't the empire doing something about it? I'm sure they would once they discovered that their transport had been taken and their crew captured and killed, although I wasn't sure how quickly that would be tracked back to the Xulonians if they used slavers as intermediaries.

"Why not transfer their citizens to these moons?" I asked.

"A logical suggestion, but I believe the collective that operates them is making such profit from the moons that they won't stop. Not to mention, I'm sure the citizens have become addicted to the escape of the avatars."

"Who wouldn't want to escape the reality of a polluted planet full of assholes and go kill some innocent aliens who look nothing like you?" I grumbled.

"Not all the moons are hunting moons. Only this one. The others are..." he paused, and his spikes flushed, "...quite different."

"If there aren't armed hunters chasing you on the other ones, then different still sounds better." Then I glanced quickly at the alien. "Not that I'm not pleased to have met you."

Baboo chuckled. "You don't offend me, human, although I would be very careful what you wish for when it comes to the Xulonian moons. I do not think Torst would want you to be on another moon," Baboo added, glancing up at me with a shy smile. "Especially not the lust one."

My face warmed. "I think you're right about that."

"You have been mates for a long time?"

I bit back a laugh. "No." How did I explain that we weren't really mates, at least not in the formal sense of the word? I couldn't exactly say that I'd screwed the Taori so he wouldn't go mad with mating fever. "It's been more recent."

He tilted his head at me, waiting for me to explain.

"I've only known him since I was dumped on this moon, and he saved me. Things happened pretty quickly after that."

"I see." The tips of Baboo's brown spikes were flaming red.

"I doubt we'd ever have ended up together if it wasn't for this crazy situation."

He walked for a few more steps before glancing up at me. "I don't know about that. I have noticed the way he looks at you.

He seems very serious about protecting you. It's why we are searching for your friend together."

I blew out a breath. "Was it that obvious?"

"The Taori seem very powerful, but I do not think subtly is one of their great strengths."

I grinned at the small alien. "Well put."

"If he did not view you as his mate, he would not care so much about Rafe." He let out a high-pitched giggle. "Not that he should worry. Rafe would never act on his flirtation."

Again, I experienced an unwanted thrill that Torst had staked his claim on me and an equally powerful burst of irritation. The last thing I should want after fighting to be independent and viewed as a capable security officer was to be seen as a male's property. Torst's possessiveness should make me want to punch him in the gut instead of making me want to curl up against his warm chest.

Maybe the alien moon was messing with my mind—or my hormones—because reacting this way to any guy going all cavemen over me was completely out of character. If any of my girlfriends acted like this, I'd have smacked them in the face and told them to get a grip. But Torst had saved my life, and I had been the reason his mating fever hadn't driven him insane. Those weren't the kinds of things most couples dealt with over the entire course of a relationship, much less right after meeting each other. Maybe I could give myself a pass until we escaped from the crazy hunting moon.

"I'm not worried," I said. "Rafe seems like a decent kid."

Baboo giggled again. "You should know that Rafe is the oldest of us all. He doesn't lord his age over us because among his kind, he is still considered young, but don't mistake his appearance for inexperience or true youth."

So, Torst had been right. "How old are we talking?"

"Many times my own age, and I am nearing one hundred astro-years."

I gasped at this. "That's crazy." Then I winked at Baboo. "Well, that settles it. I could never get involved with such an old guy."

Baboo rubbed his stubby fingers together in glee. "Please allow me to be there when you tell him this."

I liked this little guy more and more. "I promise."

We both turned to face forward as we rounded a bend in the tunnel, and the amber glow of light caught on something lying on the rock floor. It took my brain a few beats to comprehend what I was seeing as we drew closer to the sprawled body. When I did, I screamed.

"Val!"

CHAPTER
THIRTY-FOUR

Torst

I couldn't run ahead without losing Rafe's light or leaving him in the dust, but to the Berrian's credit, he matched my long strides as we raced through the tunnels toward the scream. My pulse jangled with the knowledge that it was Lia's scream we'd heard, and my gut clenched into a cold ball of regret that I'd sent her off with Baboo and not with Rafe.

I shifted my gaze to the pale-haired alien for a beat, cursing myself for letting petty jealousy get in the way of protecting my mate. His fire powers would have been greater protection for her. Better yet, I should have gone with her myself and let the other survivors pair off, even if it meant Lia or I would have had to cede some control.

I choked back a growl. The female was still so stubborn and willful. I'd thought the mating fever—and especially the mating clench—would have proven once and for all that I had dominance over her, but the only thing it had done was make me want her more and transform my need to protect her into a driving compulsion.

Memories of her small body bound to mine as my cock locked her to me sent fresh waves of desire crashing over me, and I fisted my hands and pumped them harder as I ran. I had to find her. If anything happened to her...

I refused to let myself finish the thought. I'd lost one mate. I couldn't lose another, even if it meant locking her to me so she would never be away from my sight again. The thought of having my cock permanently buried in the beautiful human forced a claiming growl from my lips.

Rafe glanced at me with wide, questioning eyes. "I never thought I'd hear that sound up close."

I ignored him and kept running by his side. The shadows of our pumping legs and swinging arms cavorted across the rock walls and ceiling, seeming to be both ahead of us and behind at the same time depending on how Rafe held the light. Since the scream, there had been no other sounds but that of our thundering footfall and heaving breaths. I didn't allow myself to dwell on what the scream had meant or why there had been only one.

We rounded a bend, the light making the turn before us and melding with more light.

"Up ahead!" Rafe said, pointing to the faint glow coming from the end of a long stretch.

I grunted my acknowledgement, and we both ran even faster, the flames flaring brighter in Rafe's hand.

At the end of the straightaway, voices reached us over our own noisy approach. I snatched the blade from my waistband. The voices sounded low and calm—and not like the Xulonians or the mercenaries I'd heard—but I didn't want to run into a potential battle unprepared.

Rafe nodded at me, then a second ball of fire spun into existence in his other hand. One for light, I suspected, and one for attack. I returned his nod.

"Into the valley of death ride the Ten Thousand," I whispered to myself from habit, the battle litany firing my blood and calming my soul simultaneously. "We are the Taori. We are the Immortals."

"Let's do this," Rafe added in his own determined voice.

When we made another turn, we both nearly stumbled to a stop and fell over Baboo as he knelt on the ground. For a moment, I thought he was bending over Lia, but she knelt across from him, her gaze trained on the woman lying prone on the ground.

Relief washed over me when I saw that Lia was safe and unharmed. Then I noticed her frown.

"Do you think you two could have made more noise getting here?"

Baboo bobbed his head, glancing at us. "It sounded like the approach of a herd of landu beasts."

Rafe coughed out a laugh. "And here we were running to save you."

"I heard you scream," I said to Lia, the words sounding weak even to my own ears. "I thought..."

Her expression softened as she straightened to stand next to me and slipped her hand into mine. "I'm fine. Val isn't."

Some of the tension I'd been holding seeped from me as I closed my hand around hers, the touch of her skin on mine like a balm on my heart. I peered down at the human female with waves of dark hair spilling across the rock. "You found her."

"She's alive," Lia said, "but she's not conscious, and we don't know why."

Now Rafe was bending down next to Baboo, and the small, brown-skinned alien tipped his head up to us. "I detect no obvious injuries."

"Her skin is cool," Rafe said, brushing his fingertips across her forehead. "Maybe she's been wandering in the tunnels by herself. They can get cold."

He rubbed his hands together and a warm, amber light glowed between them. Then he placed his hands above her, moving them in tandem down the length of her body. As we watched, the woman began to stir, moving her head from side to side and moaning.

"It's working," Lia whispered, her voice quivering with anticipation. "She's going to be okay."

As Rafe passed his palms above her, Val's eyes fluttered open. She blinked lazily several times, her dark eyes unfocused as she regained consciousness. Then her eyes flew wide, and she started babbling incoherently.

"Is that your human language?" I asked Lia, when my universal translator failed to convert the sounds into any comparable words.

She shook her head and bit the corner of her thumbnail. "Not any I've ever heard, and Val and I always spoke English together, so I'm not sure what this is." She slipped her hand from mine, and knelt next to her shipmate, taking the woman's hand. "Val. It's me, Lia. From the imperial transport. Do you remember?"

Val's gaze locked onto Lia, and she stopped babbling. She tilted her head as if trying to place her, took a deep, shaky breath and nodded. Then she slid her gaze from Lia to Baboo and Rafe and finally to me. When she saw me, her eyes widened again, and her mouth went slack. Then they rolled into the back of her head, and her body went limp.

Lia craned her neck to look over her shoulder at me. "Did you scowl at her?"

Rafe peered up at me. "Maybe it was the horns and tats. He's intimidating before you get to know him. Even then..."

I grunted brusquely, pushing them aside as I bent to scoop up the female, my gaze hesitating for a moment as I caught a glimpse of something familiar. "I didn't scowl at her. She's probably weak and needs food."

Baboo stood. "He's right. We should get her back to the gathering place."

As we moved back through the tunnel with Rafe and Baboo in the lead, I stole a quick look behind us, hoping I'd been wrong about what I'd seen and jerking my head forward when I saw that I wasn't.

The tuft of dark hair that had been beside Val had undoubtably come from a Taori tail. One of my brothers had been there with the female—and left.

CHAPTER
THIRTY-FIVE

Lia

Torst was silent on the walk back, although it wasn't completely uncharacteristic, especially since Rafe and Baboo were chattering the entire way. I kept sneaking glances at him and then at Val. She was still out, but she'd definitely reacted to Torst before she'd fainted. Was it like Rafe had suggested? Had Val been startled by his appearance—the wild hair, silver-striped horns, and dark tattoos—or was it something else?

There was no way Val had seen Torst before, was there? I'd only encountered him after I left her in the cave, and he'd been with me every moment since. I shook the thoughts from my mind. I was jumping to conclusions and allowing my mind to conjure the worst possibilities—a habit I'd had since childhood when imagining the worst outcomes would help steel me for the reality, which, when I was ill, often wasn't much better.

But Torst didn't deserve my doubt. He'd done nothing to earn the niggling voice in my head reminding me that I really knew little about the alien. He was the strong, silent type. So what? That didn't mean I couldn't trust him. I'd been trusting him with my life since he'd first saved me. I had no reason to stop now.

Then why did Val freak out when she saw him? What did she know that I didn't? The questions continued to swirl through my brain until we reached the wide opening in the tunnels and all the alcoves around it. Zennen and the other aliens rushed forward when they saw us, and the tall leader waved Torst into his own alcove when he spotted Val limp in his arms.

"Is that your friend?" He wrung his hands as she was lowered onto his grass-stuffed mattress.

"That's Val. She was unconscious when we found her, and she only came to briefly after Rafe warmed her."

"Then she saw this guy," Rafe jerked a thumb at Torst, "and passed out again."

Torst narrowed his eyes at the fire starter and backed from the alcove with a grunt.

Zennen patted me on the back as his antennae quivered. "I'm sure she needs some rest and sustenance. She'll be comfortable here." He gave me a sheepish smile. "I do have the most creature comforts since I've been here so long."

Now that he pointed it out, I noticed more cushions on his mattress along with a brass tray to the side that held a water goblet and a velvet roll tied with string. "Thank you for sharing your space. You've been too kind."

"Nonsense." He fluttered a hand to wave away my thanks. "Survivors help each other. It's how we continue to survive." His gaze flicked behind me as the female with long platinum hair entered. "Now, why don't you go check on your big friend, while Yara helps me tend to the female? We were both healers on our planets, you know."

I eyed Yara as she crouched beside Val and unrolled the velvet pouch from Zennen's tray that was filled with small, brown bottles and glass tubes with cork stoppers. "Do you know how to heal humans?"

Yara glanced back at me with a warm smile as she held up a metallic pouch in her gloved hands. "First, we will hydrate her. Then I will see if she needs any of Zennen's oils. I promise we won't damage your friend."

I released a heavy breath. "Thank you." Then I backed out, leaving Val in their hands.

Torst wasn't gathered around the glowing flames with the others, and for a moment, I feared he might have returned to the tunnels. But then I saw that the curtain draping our alcove was down, and I poked my head inside.

Torst sat on the edge of the mattress with his arms looped around his knees and his head bowed. I wondered if he might be sleeping, but he jerked up and met my gaze with his own blue eyes that almost glowed through the dimness.

Stepping inside all the way, I left a crack in the curtain for light. "Do you want to tell me what happened back there?"

I wasn't sure what I was hoping to get from him, but I had to ask.

His brow furrowed. "What do you mean?"

"I mean, why did Val seem to recognize you and panic?"

His face spasmed for such a brief moment I might have imagined it. "I don't know. I've never seen the woman before, unless you count seeing you both in the distance as you ran away from the Xulonian hunters."

This was new. "You saw us running from the hunters?"

"It was soon after I freed myself from the escape pod. I was still figuring out where I was when I saw you two being chased. I didn't know you were being hunted or that this was a staged hunting moon, so I suspected you might be criminals on the run."

I couldn't help laughing at this as I remembered his odd questions when he'd caught me. "That's why you asked me what I'd done to deserve being chased. I don't think Val or I would make good criminals." Then I remembered what I'd been asking him. "That was the only time you saw Val?"

He nodded before tilting his head as he peered at me. "You think I had something to do with her vanishing? You think I'm lying to you?"

The hurt in his voice was palpable, and I instantly felt like a complete jerk. There was no way he could have had anything to do with Val disappearing, since he'd been busy saving my ass, and we'd been inseparable since then. Not only that, but he'd given me zero reason to doubt him and a thousand reasons to trust him with my life. I knew in my gut that Torst was honorable and good, which meant there was another explanation for Val's reaction—one I'd have to wait to learn when she woke. Until then, Torst was the same Taori who'd been by my side and, most recently, in my bed.

"Of course not." I closed the distance between us. "I know you didn't—you couldn't."

Torst pulled me down so that I was straddling him with my knees on either side of his hips. Even though I'd spent a considerable amount of time with him inside me, I was overcome by a sudden bout of shyness. Torst was no longer wild with mating fever, and I wasn't sure if the calm, non-feverish version of him even wanted me like that. Once the fever had passed, did the Taori still crave the females they'd been desperate for earlier, or was all the desire and longing and dominant words just the mating fever talking?

Torst reached up and pulled my hair from its ponytail, then he tangled his fingers in my loose strands. "I need you, Lia."

I drew in an abrupt breath. "Is the mating fever back?"

He spread his fingers across the back of my head and pulled me closer to him, his lips hovering over mine. "No, your body quenched me like nothing else ever has, but that doesn't mean I don't still desire you." He tipped my head back so he could skim his lips up my neck and nip my earlobe. "It doesn't mean I don't want to bury myself inside you, Lia, and hear your moans of pleasure."

My heart spasmed and my pulse thrummed wildly. "You don't... I mean... you do?"

He pulled back, his gaze pinning me. "Do you?"

I nodded without even pausing to think about it. I'd never felt more alive than when he'd been inside me, and I'd never felt as powerful or sexy as when I'd been taking all of him. Then I thought about the sounds of his mating and the aliens sitting right outside the curtain. I couldn't even pretend they were asleep this time. I cut my gaze to the opening in the curtain. "What about...?"

Torst wrapped his other arm around my back and flipped me over so that I was under him on the mattress. "This time I want to go slow and savor you, mate. You are as fragrant as a field of myrrah flowers, and each sweet kiss is better than any ale."

His words sent a warm pulse down my spine. "You didn't talk like that last night."

"There is mating fever, and then there is the Taori language of love."

My heart quivered. Love?

Torst's face was in shadows as he hovered above me, but the

thin circle of iridescent blue around his dark pupils held me in thrall. He feathered a kiss across my lips, desire skimming over my skin like electricity. "I devour each of your kisses like the sweetest sugar."

My only answer was a whimper as he crushed his mouth to mine.

CHAPTER
THIRTY-SIX

Torst

I swallowed her moans as I kissed her, my tongue stroking hers as I deepened the motion. The taste of her was so heady the universe shifted beneath me, as if the moon had slipped on its axis and spun off course.

The mating fever had consumed me with a driving, pounding need to claim her and fill her. It had been lust and desire burning in my veins that had subsumed all rational thought and banished reason or caution. Nothing had existed for me but claiming Lia and locking her to me with the mating clench until she'd been filled by my seed and the fever had been extinguished.

But now...

I tore my lips from her and snatched an eager breath before dragging my tongue down the length of her throat. Now I wanted to take my time and let myself be consumed by her, not the Quaibyn. I wanted to drown in her sweet taste and soft sounds, and revel in pleasuring her. Now that my feverish compulsion to fuck her hard and fast had passed, I needed to feel her—and feel the connection growing between us.

I couldn't deny the bond that was stronger than just the afterglow of mating fever, and more than the result of being locked together by the clench. The more I saw of the female's inner strength and courage, the more I was drawn to her. It didn't hurt that her body ignited a fire within me, and her velvet heat was intoxicating.

"Torst," she gasped, running her hands down my bare chest and tugging at my pants.

I put a finger to her lips. "Shh." Her urgent movements stilled, and she peered at me, her chest heaving. "Do you trust me, little one?"

She nibbled her bottom lip and nodded. With a quick grunt, I raised her arms over her head and then pulled her shirt up and over them, tossing it to the floor. I bit my own lip to keep from releasing a growl of pleasure when I saw her dusky nipples harden in the cool air, the skin around them pebbling. I wanted nothing more than to devour them, but I focused my attention on her pants, unfastening them and tugging them off, along with her panties, and throwing them to the floor.

When she was lying naked beneath me, her perfect body rising and falling with each breath and her eyes wide with anticipation, I took her by the hips and flipped her over. Then I pulled her up onto all fours, and she rocked back with a sigh.

I dug my hands into her hips and leaned over her. "Do you want my cock?"

She released another sigh, this one dripping with need.

"Not yet," I told her, giving her bare ass a small slap. "Not until I've gotten my fill of you."

Then I spread her legs and dropped down on my back until my head was beneath her and her knees were over my shoulders. Reaching behind, I grabbed her ass cheeks and tilted her forward until my mouth was on her sex.

Lia's own mouth fell open, and she dropped her head back, as I dragged my tongue through her, dipping into her opening and stroking it like I had her tongue. The groan that slipped from her lips echoed around us, and I swirled my tongue deep within her before pulling away.

"You rode my cock," I whispered to her in the darkened alcove. "Now I want you to ride my tongue. Can you do that for me?"

She nodded desperately, raking a hand through her hair as I found her slick nub with the tip of my tongue. My view was incredible as I looked upon her naked body and greedily licked her. She moved languidly above me, rocking her hips back and forth so that her perfect, small breasts bounced slightly. Her eyes were closed, and her lower lip pulled between her teeth as if to keep another sound from escaping. But I didn't need her sweet noises to know that I was pleasuring her. I could taste her arousal on my tongue as I worked it inside her and then swirled it over the swollen bundle of nerves that made her quiver.

I curled my tail around her body so I could use the velvety tip to caress her nipples, one after the other. Lia's rocking became quicker, and I matched it with my mouth, grasping her ass cheeks to keep my tongue on her. She fell forward, bracing her arms over my head as her body trembled and my face was buried in her hot flesh. Then she moved her hands to my horns, stroking her fingers down the stripes and making my pulse spike. If she wanted to play, I could show her how Taori played.

I slid my tail around and stroked her opening while I sucked her nub. Her eyes flew open as I slowly pushed it inside her, the rounded end sliding in easily. She twisted her head around to watch my tail stroke in and out, and her tight heat clenched around me.

"I've never..." her words trailed off as she rolled her head back to me.

"Taken a tail before?" I asked when I pulled my lips from her clit for a breath. "Do you like it as much as your eyes tell me you do?"

Her answer was a hum that became a moan as she rocked back to meet the thrust of my tail.

The velvety tip of my tail was not as thick as my cock, but the sensation of being inside her and licking her at the same time sent a possessive rumble through my chest. The sound buzzed my lips and her slick flesh.

She sucked in a shocked breath at the vibration before her entire body tensed and she threw her head back, her legs clenching around my head and blocking out all sound. There was only the rushing of blood in my ears, as I held her to me and felt the pleasure pulse through her and squeeze my tail.

When she stopped shaking, I moved my hands from her ass, yanking my own pants down hard and freeing my aching cock. Tasting her sweet arousal and feeling her explode on my tongue and around my tail had made my cock rock hard. I stroked my hand down the length of it, bumping the three crowns. I slid my tail from her before grasping her hips and moving her down so that my cock was notched at her entrance. Lia's breathing was ragged as I hesitated.

"More?" I asked, my voice hushed. "Or was being fucked by my tail enough, little female?"

She shook her head as if she was delirious. "More."

With a contented growl, I drove her down on my cock until she'd taken me to the hilt. Lia arched back as her body adjusted around me. Even as soaked as she was for me, her body sheathed my cock so tightly I had to fight to keep from exploding.

"So perfect for me," I whispered, licking her delicious juices from my own lips as I lifted her up and down on my shaft.

Even though she was human, she *was* perfect for me. Being inside her was euphoric and made me feel more complete than I'd ever been. The intensity of my pleasure was overshadowed for a moment by a pang of guilt.

The connection I felt to Lia was even stronger than the one I'd had to Kaolin so long ago. I'd pledged never to forget my intended—and I never had—but I'd mourned her for long enough. She never would have wished for me to be alone and empty for so many astro-years. She would not have wanted my love to morph into a hate and thirst for vengeance that had consumed me. Now, for the first time in as long as I could remember, I desired something more than revenge. I wanted to save Lia and build a future with her.

My heart squeezed as I gazed up at the unlikely object of my affection, her dark hair wild around her face. She had no horns and no tail, but she was as beautiful to me as any female from Taor. And she was mine. That I felt without a shadow of a doubt. I was no longer a young, impulsive warrior. I was a Taori who'd known heartache and loss. I knew my heart, and as mystifying as it was, Lia had captured it.

With a dark, dominant growl, I knifed up and flipped her over onto her back, covering my body with hers and stroking my cock deep as I held her with my eyes. I focused every dormant desire and long-stifled passion in my gaze, claiming her body and soul as I peered deep into her heart.

Fucking her feverishly had been something that would be burned into my mind forever, but this claiming had clenched my soul. As I exploded hot into her and released the past, I caught her mouth in a kiss to keep myself from bellowing loud enough to bring the cave down around us.

CHAPTER
THIRTY-SEVEN

Lia

I woke up with a sated sigh of contentment. I hadn't meant to fall asleep, but the combination of searching the tunnels and sex with Torst had made it easy to succumb after we'd collapsed in a sweaty heap on the mattress. His heavy breathing and the rhythmic rising and falling of his chest had been like a sedative, as I'd basked in the afterglow of what had been an entirely different experience than the feverish release of Torst's mating fever. Not that I'd minded the mating fever, and I especially hadn't minded the fever clench that had held me to him long after most guys would have rolled away.

But this had been different. He had been different. And the way he'd looked at me just before he'd come had been so intense tears had stung the backs of my eyes. The Taori may claim that he couldn't bewitch me with his iridescent blue eyes, but I wasn't sure I believed him.

Missing the heat of his substantial body, I reached for Torst, and my arm flopped onto nothing, the dried grass in the mattress crunching.

I sat up and scanned the shady alcove. No Torst.

"Not this again," I muttered, as I hurriedly pulled on my clothes. I wasn't worried that the fever had come back, and he was wandering around naked and horny. For one, his clothes were gone. But I couldn't ignore that he'd been quiet since we'd found Val. Even the usual grunts and growls that made up most of his conversations had faded into silence. Something was worrying him. Something he wasn't telling me.

The thought that the Taori might be keeping secrets from me hurt. We might not have known each other for long, but we'd been thrust into a crazy situation and even forced to be lovers. I'd told him everything, even sharing with him that I'd been sick as a kid, which wasn't something I normally told people I'd just met. But Torst had been different, and he'd made me feel like I could trust him with my life and my heart. Dark fingers of doubt curled treacherously around my heart even as I tried to shake off the uncertainty. Maybe, despite his sweet words, he didn't feel the same way about me.

"Talk is cheap." I repeated the phrase I'd heard from my mother so many times. She'd drummed into me the importance of watching people's actions instead of believing their words. As much as I hated to admit that my mother had been right, learning about others through their acts and not their empty claims had served me well.

Pulling my hair up into a high ponytail, I swept the curtain aside and stepped into the central gathering area. The hovering ball of fire remained burning, like it always did, but there were no survivors sitting around it on the makeshift log benches and seats. Had everyone left?

Panic fluttered in my chest, the old childhood fear of being left behind rearing its head. Then I glanced to Zennen's quarters, spotting Val sleeping soundly and the tall, lavender-skinned alien sitting beside her with his eyes closed and his antennae gently bowed as he leaned against the wall. At least everyone wasn't gone, I thought with a measure of relief.

When I heard a muffled grunt, I swung my head around, my gaze honing in on one of the tunnels. That had been one of Torst's grunts. Even though the tunnel was dark, I had a sinking feeling he was inside it.

The curtain covering Rafe's alcove was pulled across it, which meant he was likely asleep. It also meant I couldn't convince him to give me some light so I could follow Torst. Not that I knew how to hold a fireball. Baboo had used his tele-kinetic powers to keep the one we'd had aloft. I had no such powers.

I peered back at the tunnel I was convinced Torst had gone into without me, my irritation growing. Why would he have gone without me? Why would he have gone without any of us? All the survivors had agreed to search for Val and his fellow Taori warriors. Now that we'd located Val, I was certain no one would object to helping him find his friends. My mind returned to the nagging feeling that he was keeping something from me, and my gut churned.

"Screw this." I curled my hands into fists and strode into the tunnel after him, fueled by my hurt and my anger.

Almost as soon as I'd walked a few steps, the light from the flames faded, and the gaping blackness swallowed me. I put a hand to one wall to guide me, my own footsteps and quick breaths the only sounds as I moved deeper down the path and farther from the warmth of the gathering area.

"What the hell are you doing, Lia?" I whispered to myself, as much to hear another voice as anything. I didn't even hear Torst's guttural sounds, and the churning in my gut intensified as I second-guessed my decision to barrel after him.

Impulsive.

I frowned as I thought of the word my mother had used like a curse when she heard I'd joined the military academy and then again when I told her about my posting as a security officer. But what she'd always deemed impulsive, I'd thought of as brave. Rushing into danger was the only way I could deal with fear. Cowering and waiting for death wasn't living, and once I wasn't sick, I'd promised myself that I would finally live.

Maybe my tendency to run headfirst into danger hadn't always worked for me—I *was* stranded on an alien moon being hunted for sport—but it was better than the alternative. Besides, Torst was even more reckless than I was, which was probably why we'd both entered a dark tunnel alone. If he was in here.

Just as I was suspecting that the grunt I'd heard hadn't been Torst, and I'd barreled into the darkness for no good reason, I heard it again. The curt growl was up ahead, and it definitely came from the Taori. I picked up my pace, jogging on my toes to catch up to him.

"Torst?"

A low rumble filled the tunnel, and it didn't sound pleased. I rounded a corner and ran smack into something huge and hard, stumbling back and landing on my ass.

"Ow! Duck me. That hurt."

Strong hands picked me up and held me by the sides of my arms. "Lia?"

"Of course, it's Lia," I grumbled, brushing off my dusty ass even though I still couldn't see a thing in the pitch-darkness. "What other woman would chase you into a dark tunnel?"

"Or say duck?" he muttered. "Why did you follow me?"

"Why did you run?"

"I didn't run." He sounded offended as he dropped my arms. I couldn't help myself from cocking my head, even though

201

he couldn't see my look of disbelief. "I woke up and you were gone. You're in a dark tunnel alone heading away from the rest of the survivors, and I'm guessing you didn't tell anyone you were leaving. What would you call that?"

Another grunt followed by a huff of breath. "I wanted to tell you."

"Tell me what?"

"About my suspicions—my fears."

Well, that was vague. "I have no idea what you're talking about, Torst, but you've been acting off since we found Val. Does this have to do with why she reacted to you?"

"I'm not sure, but it might. I was telling you the truth when I said that I'd never seen your shipmate before—aside from spotting you two running from the hunters. I haven't, but that doesn't mean she hasn't encountered another Taori."

I flinched at this. "But if another of your kind found her, why wasn't he with her in the tunnel?"

"I don't know the answer to that, but I do believe he's been in the tunnels, which is why I had to come looking for him."

I rubbed my own arms briskly as the skin pebbled. "You came down this dark, cold tunnel by yourself on a hunch?"

"Not a hunch. When we found your friend, I spotted a tuft of what I recognized as Taori tail fur near her."

A flash of amber light illuminated the tunnel, revealing Rafe standing behind me, holding a spinning ball of flames. "Sounds like you've both been keeping secrets."

THIRTY-EIGHT

Torst

"Rafe!" Lia pressed a hand to her heart. "Don't sneak up on us like that."

His youthful expression hardened for a moment. "You accuse me of sneaking when you two were conspiring in the dark?"

"Conspiring?" My tail twitched behind me, a tell that I was agitated.

Lia stepped between us with one palm facing each of our chests. "Why don't we dial back the testosterone, boys?" She pivoted to Rafe. "There's no conspiring going on. Torst went looking for the fellow Taori he thinks are also stranded on the moon, and I followed him."

Rafe narrowed his gaze at me, as if he wasn't convinced by this explanation. "Why come alone and in the dark? You know I would have come with you if you asked."

The subtle break in his voice told me that the alien wasn't angry, he was hurt.

I opened my mouth to speak, but he continued before I could.

"I thought we made a decent team when we searched the tunnels earlier." He met my gaze. "I thought we were friends, or on our way to being fr—"

"Rafe," I said sharply, cutting him off. "I didn't leave you behind because I didn't value you as a teammate. Our meeting was written in the stars along with the battles we will fight in as brothers."

His mouth gaped, and Lia grinned at his speechlessness.

"I didn't bring anyone with me," I shot Lia a pointed look, "because I didn't want to risk any of you."

"We know the risks." Rafe flicked one hand through his messy hair. "I've been on this moon longer than either of you. If there's anyone who knows how to avoid the hunters, it's one of the survivors like me."

Lia glanced at me, inclining her head at the fire starter as if telling me to spill the rest.

"It isn't the hunters on the surface I wish to protect you all from, or even the new mercenaries. It's my Taori brothers."

Rafe shifted the ball of flames from one palm to the other. "You think your own kinsmen are a threat?"

"Not in usual circumstances." I drew in a breath, hesitating before telling him what I knew might change his feelings toward me and my welcome with the other survivors. "As you know, my Taori sky ship was sucked here through a temporal wormhole and then destroyed by the Xulonians. What you don't know is that the temporal flux affected me and my fellow Taori in an unusual way. The males of our species have always been afflicted by what we call the Quaibyn, the mating fever."

Rafe's eyebrows popped high, and he darted a glance at Lia.

"Normally, the Quaibyn only occurs once every decade or so. It is an occurrence we expect, so our home world has priestesses dedicated to servicing the fever. Even on our journey through the stars, we have been able to adjust our course to intercept planets with houses of hedonism."

"Until you went through the wormhole?" Rafe asked.

I nodded. "Your impatience burns as brightly as the fire in your hands, but yes. The temporal energy seems to have sped up the Quaibyn."

The alien eyed me. "Do you have it now?"

"No, my mating fever has been cured."

Rafe swung his gaze to Lia, a grin splitting his face. She glared at him, even though she shifted from one foot to the other.

I folded my arms over my bare chest, emitting a growl that snapped his gaze back to me.

"Sorry," he stammered. "It just explains a lot."

"I may no longer be suffering from mating fever, but I fear the other Taori were not as lucky as I was to find a perfect mate." Especially if the Taori who'd also landed on the moon was Daiken.

Rafe bobbed his head up and down as he tapped one foot on the stone floor. "So, you're afraid that there are more Taori on our moon, just as big and scary as you but a lot hornier?"

"The mating fever is more than sexual desire," I said. "It's a driving compulsion that overpowers logical thought or self-control. A Taori male who is deep in the throes of mating fever would do anything to obtain a female."

Rafe looked at Lia again. "Even one who's already...?"

I scowled at this, and the thought of another male—especially one of my Taori brothers—touching Lia sent a prickling heat skittering across my skin. "The Quaibyn affects each male differently and with various intensity. Usually, it slackens its hold after many cycles, but I have no idea how the temporal energy has altered it, only to say that it has quickened the approach."

"Which means time might be running out to find the other Taori?"

I gave the alien a single, solemn nod before adding, "And I have reason to believe one has made his way into the tunnels."

Rafe tilted his head to me in unspoken question.

"There was a remnant of Taori tail fur next to the human we found unconscious."

The alien let out a low whistle, and it echoed down the rock path. "That explains a lot."

"The human female appeared untouched, her clothes were intact, and there were no defensive marks on her skin. I am fairly certain she hadn't been accosted, but I cannot explain why there would be evidence of a Taori next to her unconscious body. I only know we need to track him down before he returns in full mating fever."

"Then it sounds like you need all the help you can get." Rafe rocked back on his heels. "This moon is bigger than you'd expect, and you've only seen a fraction of the environments. If you want to stand a chance of finding your shipmates, you need someone who knows the moon and the tunnels."

I mulled this over, hating how right the cocky alien was. "I can't ask you to put yourself in danger. This is my responsibility."

Rafe shook his head. "The only way to stay alive on this moon is to work together. No one makes it if they go it alone."

"Exactly what I've been trying to tell this stubborn Taori since I met him," Lia said from the corner of her mouth.

I swiveled to face her. "Even if I accept Rafe's help, I can't allow you to be in harm's way." Before she could begin the indignant protests that were obviously on the tip of her tongue,

I held up a hand. "The Taori defend their true mates to the death, gladly welcoming its caresses to protect the honor of the female bound to their soul. If my Taori brother came for you to quench his fever, I would be compelled to send him beyond the veil to the shadowlands. Please don't force that fate on me."

Her mouth went slack, and then she clamped it shut, nodding silently.

Rafe cleared his throat. "I've heard enough tales about Taori honor to believe what you've told me, but this needs to be shared with the others. The danger extends to all of the survivors."

As much as I'd wished to handle the matter without involving the others, he was right. If my Taori brother had already been in the tunnels, and he was experiencing the Quaibyn, everyone underground was in danger.

"Then we should return to the gathering place," I said. "It appears I have a tale to share."

Lia slipped her hand into mine and squeezed. "We'll do it together."

My heart constricted as her touch sent a possessive fire through me, even as a cold certainty settled in the pit of my stomach. I would eagerly embrace death to keep her safe—or hasten the journey to the shadowland of anyone who dared touch her. Even a Taori.

THIRTY-NINE

Lia

"Why did you keep this from us?" Zennen asked Torst once he'd explained the Quaibyn to the survivors as they sat around the fire. Shadows stretched across the ceiling and up the walls as the group stared at us, transfixed by Torst's tale of the fever.

Torst bowed his head. "My plan was always to leave before it became noticeable or dangerous. I didn't want to risk any of you, but I also didn't want to scare you. The Taori are honorable warriors. We would never knowingly put others at risk."

"He tried to leave," I said, the quaver in my voice revealing my nerves. "I'm the one who insisted he stay."

All eyes swiveled to me.

"Then it is you who were reckless with our hospitality." Zennen's expression conveyed the depth of his disappointment, and hot shame washed over me.

I lowered my gaze to the floor, biting the inside of my mouth to keep my lips from trembling.

"The only thing she was reckless with was her own safety," Torst said. "Lia gave herself to me to break the fever's grip. She not only saved me from madness, but she also saved my life."

The heat in my cheeks faded, even though I could still feel the gazes on me. I cut my eyes to Torst and gave him a grateful smile.

Rafe raised a hand. "I can vouch for some kind of mating fever being burned off between these two. My alcove is next to theirs."

Yara giggled and nodded. "And mine is on the other side."

Zennen straightened, frowning at the levity. "How do we know that this fever won't return?"

Torst locked eyes with me, the shimmering blue irises holding my gaze in a trance. "The mating clench bound us together body and soul. Once it released us, the Quaibyn was gone."

Rafe let out a low whistle as Torst and I stared at each other as if our gaze was a lifeline. "I don't think any of us doubt your bond. I would tell you to get a room, but I know how much good that does."

I wrenched my gaze from the Taori and gave Rafe a sharp look, which only made him laugh.

Zennen cleared his throat. "I suppose we can forgive this omission since the danger is gone."

"It was never my intention to stay long enough for any of you to be at risk," Torst said.

"And I was never going to let him go mad," I added. "Not after he'd saved my life more than once."

Torst smiled at me as his gaze held mine again, the intensity of his eyes almost stealing my breath. The sex was incredible, but the way he looked at me was even more intimate.

"I was saved by one like him, too."

There were murmurs around the fire as we all turned toward the soft voice. Val stood in the entrance to Zennen's alcove, with one hand braced on the stone wall for support.

I jumped up and rushed to her, looping an arm around her waist for support. "You're awake."

She smiled at me then swept her gaze around the aliens sitting around the hovering ball of flames that sent up no smoke. "I feel like I missed some things."

I laughed as I helped her to one of the log seats. "These are all fellow survivors who've managed to stay hidden from the hunters. They took me and Torst in when we happened upon their underground tunnels."

Val pushed a dark curl off her forehead and rubbed a hand across it. "I was in a tunnel."

I took the seat next to her and leaned forward. "That's where we found you—in a tunnel. Do you remember how you got there?"

Her gaze slid to Torst, and she bit her lower lip. "A huge creature with horns and a tail dragged me into the tunnel."

Torst grunted, his jaw clenching and a vein on his neck throbbing. This clearly wasn't what he wanted to hear.

As everyone around us shifted nervously, Val shook her head. "I don't mean he dragged me against my will. He saved me."

I rested a hand on her knee. "You're going to have to explain. The last time I saw you was inside the cave. I went out to forage for food, and you promised to sit tight because of your ankle."

"I did sit tight, but then there were a lot of noises outside the cave, as if something was crashing through the jungle. I scooted back as far as I could and bumped into a pile of foliage. Only it wasn't a pile of leaves and vines. It was a creature who'd hidden in the cave before we got there and covered himself so he wouldn't be seen if someone looked inside."

"It worked," I said under my breath. I remembered the mound of blue foliage, but it hadn't even occurred to me that a creature could be under it.

"When I realized there was something hard and warm under the leaves, I started to panic. That was when he clamped his hand over my mouth and dragged me farther back into the cave."

I snuck a glance at Torst, wondering if he was remembering slapping a hand over my mouth to keep me quiet.

"It turned out that the farther back he dragged me, the farther back the cave went, until I realized we were going down into some sort of underground tunnel." Val let out a breath. "It was so dark, I don't think he even knew the tunnel was back there until we backed up enough."

"If it was so dark, how do you know it was a Taori who took you?" Torst asked.

Val's cheeks flushed faintly. "I couldn't see him, but I could feel him. He was massive, and all muscle with no shirt." Her gaze flitted to Torst's heavily tattooed chest. "Like you." The corner of her mouth quirked up. "And he had horns and a tail."

I cocked my head at her. "You felt all this in the dark?"

"Once we were deep inside the tunnel, he took his hand off my mouth and told me that he wasn't going to hurt me. He warned me that there were aliens on the surface with weapons." She shuddered. "He didn't seem to know where he was or why, so I explained as much as I knew about the moon and why we were being hunted."

Torst grunted and dragged a hand roughly through his hair. "He didn't remember how he came to be on the moon?"

Val shook her head. "He seemed disoriented, but I thought

he might be sick. His skin was burning hot, and he was panting like he'd been chased for a long time.

Torst stood abruptly and started pacing behind us. Val glanced nervously at him, but I gave her leg a reassuring pat. "What else do you remember?"

"My memories are hazy because it was dark and my ankle still hurt badly, but I remember him laying me down gently on the ground and telling me he had to leave me. I think I panicked about being left in the dark because I remember grabbing for him. That's when I felt his horns and when he wrapped his tail around me."

Torst's pace increased, and his fists were tight by his sides. The survivors around the fire exchanged worried looks, but no one dared interrupt Val's story.

"Did he," I hesitated as I searched for the right word, "try anything?"

Val's brow furrowed. "No, but he did lean close to my neck and smell me. At least, that's what it felt like. Then he jerked himself away from me and said he had to leave to keep me safe. I remember telling him that there were hunters on the surface, but he said death was better than dishonor, whatever that meant."

A low rumble accompanied Torst's question. "Did he give you his name?"

Val twisted to meet his gaze. "Daiken of the Immortal Army of the Taori."

The agonized groan that came from Torst sent chills down my spine.

CHAPTER
FORTY

Torst

As soon as the human said Daiken's name, my spine tensed, and my skin went cold as a sound slipped from my throat. Of all the warriors to be stranded on a hunting moon with me, why did it have to be the Taori already deep in the grip of the Quaibyn? He'd been sedated while we'd been on the Drexian battleship and when we returned him to our own ship to search for a house of hedonism, but the temporal wormhole had accelerated his fever, and now he was on a hostile planet with no way to control his compulsion.

My chest tightened as I thought about my Taori brother, but then I thought about Lia and Val, and my resolve hardened. I'd had to cross galaxies and centuries to find Lia. I would not risk her safety—even for one of my own.

"Now that we know for certain that one of your fellow Taori

is here on the moon and has found the tunnels, I'm sure you want to search for him," Lia said.

I shook my head and let out a gruff sound. "We've found your missing shipmate. That is enough. We should resume plans to attack the Xulonian command center and get off the moon."

Lia's forehead wrinkled. "You don't want to find your fellow warrior? I thought that was important to you."

All eyes were on me as the aliens circled around the glowing flames grew quiet. Even Rafe's usually arrogant smirk was gone, and Baboo appeared to be holding his breath in wait for my answer.

"My Taori kinsman chose honor. I will not take that away from him." The words tasted like ash on my tongue, but it was what Daiken would have wanted. He'd learned what this moon was, and he'd chosen to leave Val and go above ground because he wanted to be killed by the hunters. He knew he didn't have much longer before the fever devoured all reason, and he slipped into madness. He'd chosen to die rather than risk harming the female. Even though it pained me to think about him being slaughtered by the red skinned aliens with their shiny bows and bad aim, he'd made the valiant choice of a Taori.

"But," Lia spluttered, looking from Val to me, "he might be killed."

"He saved me." Val's voice cracked. "Why can't we save him?"

"Because there isn't going to be anything to save soon." Rafe looked at me pointedly. "Am I right?"

I pressed my lips together and nodded. "Daiken was already afflicted by the mating fever before our ship was pulled through the wormhole. The sickness was being controlled by sedation until we could locate a ...cure. The temporal energy made his sickness even worse, and now he's stranded down here, with no way to slow the progression. It will drive him mad if it hasn't already." I gritted my teeth so I wouldn't release a roar of frustration that one of my Taori brothers would end his life in such a pointless way. "There is no saving him now."

Val put a hand to her mouth, stifling a sob.

Zennen stood and hurried over to her, putting a slender arm around her shoulders. "Why don't you lie back down? You're still recovering."

When he'd shuffled her back into his alcove, I realized that all the survivors were still staring at me, a hush hanging over the group. They probably thought I was cruel to leave my kinsman to be hunted, but only I knew that death was not the worst fate for a Taori, and madness was the not the final indignity of the Quaibyn. Beyond the madness lay what we all feared beyond anything else—mutation into the monsters we hunted. If the Quaibyn festered long enough, the Taori would morph into a Sythian. Even thinking of Daiken as one of the slavish devouring beasts made bile tease the back of my throat.

Choosing death meant he chose honor. The alternative would be a stain that would soak into his legacy like blood soaking a battlefield. I understood Daiken, and he would understand my decision.

Lia walked over to stand by my side, slipping her hand into mine. Her wordless support sent warm tingles up my arm, and my heart squeezed. At least Lia didn't think I was a monster. I could take the misunderstanding of the rest of them as long as she didn't doubt me.

"We should talk about the mission to take out the command center." Rafe broke the heavy silence as he flicked his fingers and made the fire ball in the center flame brighter.

Baboo leaned forward, his brown skin illuminated in the amber glow. "We want the element of surprise, correct?"

"I don't think we have the numbers for an all-out assault." Lia led me back to our seats around the fire. "Our priority should be sneaking in and taking out the comms systems so they can't get messages to the planet."

I shouldn't have been surprised that Lia's assessment was so sound. She was a trained military officer and a security specialist. Then I was reminded by what Rafe had said in the tunnel. Lia worked for the empire. An empire that had shattered peace treaties between planets and stood idly by while the Xulonians enslaved and killed aliens for their twisted entertainment.

In my many long years traveling across multiple galaxies, the only empire I'd come across that didn't exploit its power had been the Drexian empire. Did she have any idea about the empire to which she'd pledged her loyalty? And how loyal was she to her empire? The idea of Lia working for an empire that could be partially complicit in the Xulonian's craven destruction of my ship and death of so many innocents on their moons made the warm feeling in my chest go cold.

"You don't agree?"

I snapped my mind from its dark wanderings, realizing that Lia was talking to me. All the other survivors watched me with curious expressions. I shook off my doubt and cleared my throat. "I do agree. Once we've eliminated any way for them to call for help, we can dismantle their operation and get off this hellish moon."

Baboo rubbed his hands together. "If we want a sneak attack, we should go in through the supply building. We can take the tunnels all the way to the entrance underneath. The command center is next to it, although not connected."

"We'll have to go outside and approach the building." Rafe snapped his fingers and ignited a flame at the end of his thumb.

"If there are any guards, we'll need to take them out before they set off any alarms."

"The command center isn't heavily fortified," Baboo added. "The aliens they hunt are never here long enough to find it—or even discover it exists."

"Their power—and the uneven odds—have made them overconfident." A growl of anticipation built in my throat. "It will be their downfall."

Rafe's top lip curled. "The only fighters we should worry about are their dimensional incarnations. They may not be great shots, but they can regenerate. If they see us, they could sound an alert back on the home world."

I grunted and sat back. I hadn't thought about that. The avatars were another communications link between the moon and the planet. "We should plan our incursion for a time when the avatars aren't active."

"They rarely hunt at night." Rafe let out a mirthless laugh. "If you think they have bad aim in the daylight, you should see their attempts in the dark. They mostly gave up their sad attempts."

"Where are the avatars when they aren't hunting?" Lia asked.

Baboo folded his arms over his barrel chest. "As far as we know, the regeneration pods are in the main command center. Once the hunt is over, the dimensionals go back into the pods to ready for the next group."

My lip twitched in disgust at these aliens who'd created avatars so they could exploit and kill, all from the comfort of their home world. "Then we go in when they're in the pods and destroy them all."

"And all the equipment that keeps this twisted operation going," Lia added. "We cut off the head of the snake, and then we set the snake on fire."

I gave her an appreciative nod. She might be a small human, but she had the soul of a warrior.

Lia gave me a pointed look. "And before you even suggest I stay behind with Val, don't. I'm going with you."

"I expected nothing less, little female," I whispered to her.

Her eyes flared, and she bit her bottom lip. She did not mind being called little female as much as she claimed she did, although I was careful to ensure only she could hear me. As tough as she'd worked to become, she still thrilled at being dominated when it was just us. But when I wasn't filling her with my cock, she was as stubborn as ever.

I might not have known her long, but I knew enough to know that the only way to keep her from joining the battle would be to bind her. The mental image of Lia tied up sent a pulse of desire through me, but I ignored it. I needed to focus on the mission and on keeping Lia safe, since she insisted on barreling toward danger.

Fear fluttered in my chest at the idea of losing another mate, but I forced the thought from my mind. I would not lose Lia. I couldn't. I would choose death first.

FORTY-ONE

Lia

T rubbed my palms down the front of my pants as I crept along the tunnel behind Torst. He hadn't argued with me about coming on the mission, but he'd made me promise to follow his command and let him lead. Considering that he was twice my size and theoretically outranked me, I'd decided not to argue the point. Besides, Torst was suffering enough without me being a pain in his ass.

The big lug might not say anything, but I knew it pained him to abandon hope of saving his fellow Taori. Abandoning Daiken—even though the warrior was going mad with mating fever and would be better off dead—had affected Torst more than he would admit to the rest of the survivors. I understood the feeling of failing your friends and colleagues, and my heart ached for him.

Baboo stopped at the front of our motley procession,

holding out one arm to slow the rest of us. He gestured to some wooden slats affixed to the stone wall. "We're here."

Torst cast me a quick glance, his dark eyebrows peaked. Baboo and Rafe had led the way through the labyrinth of underground passageways, with Baboo directing us down one fork in the tunnels after another, and Rafe lighting the way. The other survivors who'd joined our war party—which included the tiny alien who spoke in sharp clicks, and Yara, who'd tied up her snowy hair—walked silently behind me. We all peered at the rough, makeshift ladder that had seen better days and then at the covered hole in the ceiling.

"We go up that?" I eyed the narrow wooden slats and then Torst's massive form. Would it even hold him?

Baboo nodded, his smile bright. "We're standing right under the rear of the Xulonian storage unit. There's an empty crate covering the hole, and we enter through that first."

My nerves jangled at the thought of being under the enemy building. "How often have you run into Xulonian soldiers on your supply runs?"

Baboo's smile faltered. "Not often. Once I get into the empty crate, I'll be able to hear if there's anyone in the unit. I'll either give you all the okay to join me or I'll come back down, and we'll wait until the soldiers leave."

"It should be nighttime, right?" I asked. "We're attacking at fifth watch so there will be fewer patrols and no avatars outside their pods."

"That is true." Baboo twitched his shoulders. "But I can't be certain that none of their soldiers are on patrol."

"It doesn't matter." Torst's voice was a deadly purr as he slipped his blade from his waistband. "Any Xulonian on patrol will be handled."

I gulped, knowing exactly what he meant by that. His meaning wasn't lost on the rest of our group either. Baboo bobbed his head up and down nervously, and Rafe's grin was laced with his obvious hunger for revenge.

Baboo turned and pulled himself up the ladder, his small, round form fading from the bright glow of Rafe's light the closer he got to the top. I held my breath when he stopped moving, only his ankles and feet visible on the highest wooden slat.

"All quiet," he called down in a stage whisper. "Come up."

Rafe held the swirling orb of fire high as one alien after another climbed up and disappeared through the opening and into the storage building. When it was down to Torst, Rafe, and me, the Taori waved me forward.

I gripped the rough wooden boards, holding on with my nails and flattening my body close to the stone wall as I started to climb. When I was almost to the top, I twisted my head around and saw the top of Torst's horns right below me. I climbed the last few rungs and was pulled through the opening by several hands from above until I was sitting on the floor of a space lined with high shelves that were stacked with crates and boxes.

When Torst emerged from the hole in the floor, he needed no assistance but quickly turned to hoist Rafe through the opening.

"I'm surprised you let me go ahead of you," I said after we'd pulled Rafe up. "I thought you'd insist on going ahead to scout out the danger."

The corners of Torst's mouth quirked. "Then I wouldn't have enjoyed the view of you from below."

I let my mouth gape and jabbed him in the middle with my elbow, even though I was secretly pleased that he wasn't wallowing in sadness. "I thought we were focused on the mission, not my ass."

"I am a warrior used to juggling tasks. I can do both." Before

I could scold him playfully or jab him again, Torst turned to the others. "I am grateful to you all for getting us to our enemy's doorstep, but if anyone wishes to stay behind during the battle, I will not blame you."

"And miss the fun part?" Rafe scoffed, shaking his head. "No way."

"I will remain as well." Baboo squared his rounded shoulders. "My talents may be useful."

I couldn't imagine a time when the ability to move matter at will wouldn't be useful, but I also heard the tremor in the alien's voice.

Torst inclined his head at him. "Your bravery will be etched in the fabric of the skies."

Rafe spun a second ball of fire into existence in his other palm, the light illuminating the towering shelves surrounding us and sending out pulses of heat. "Shall we?"

Torst nodded at him, letting Rafe take the lead with his light and sweeping one arm around me to tuck my body behind his. We moved stealthily through the rows of shelves, only the sound of our quick, shallow breaths filling the air.

The storage unit was larger than I'd anticipated, but we finally reached a door.

"Locked," Rafe murmured. He cocked his arm as if preparing to hurl one of the balls of flame at the door, but Baboo stepped forward, putting a hand on Rafe's arm before staring purposefully at the lock. The mechanism clicked and the steel door swung open.

"Where's the fun in that?" Rafe said under his breath as he winked at Baboo.

Torst stepped forward, holding up a fist as he listened.

"Did you see that?" A harsh voice came from outside the building, the sharpness distinctly Xulonian. "The door to the supply unit popped open."

My breath lodged in my throat. So much for getting to the command center without being seen.

"One of the others must not have shut it all the way," another voice said with an annoyed sigh. "Third watch is always sloppy."

"Well, we'd better close and lock it."

Torst crouched with his blade extended and his tail twitching as footsteps indicated that the two Xulonians were walking toward us. Rafe held his arms back as if gearing up to throw his fire balls, and Baboo's face was intent as he focused on the open doorway.

"Like anyone would ever try to break in," the other Xulonian grumbled. "There's no one on this moon except dimensionals and their prey."

"I wish I'd been posted on one of the other Moorla moons. Nothing good ever happens here."

The other gave a raspy laugh, getting closer to the open door and us. "You just want to watch the mating on the lust moon."

"You don't? I can't figure out why anyone would rather come here and shoot at a bunch of frail aliens."

I bristled at the word frail, since the aliens he meant were humans.

"There's only so much mating you can watch," the other replied, as the sound of their footsteps approached.

"Says you."

The words had barely left his lips when the two red-skinned aliens appeared in the doorway. Torst didn't give them a moment to react, launching himself at the closest one and tearing a gash across his throat. Blue blood spurted onto the other Xulonian, but he was already clutching his hands to his neck and gasping for breath. Within moments, he dropped to the ground.

Rafe pivoted to face Baboo, who released a breath as his expression softened. "You couldn't let me have one?"

Baboo giggled. "Apologies. I thought it would be quieter to crush his windpipe than set him on fire."

Rafe shook his head. "Quieter, maybe, but less satisfying."

We dragged the bodies inside the storage building and stepped into the darkness. The night was cool, even though the air remained thick. I'd been underground for so long, I greedily sucked in the fresh air and tipped my head back to peer at the stars peeking through the haze of the atmosphere.

Torst wiped his blade on his leather pants and then thumped a heavy hand on Rafe's shoulder. "Once we've disabled the comms and secured our escape, I promise that you can burn it all down."

In the darkness of the night, Torst's blue eyes glowed as if they were white flames, the vengeance in his expression sending a shiver of unease down my spine and making me wonder for the briefest of moments if his fever had truly passed.

FORTY-TWO

Torst

I inhaled the scent of the moon, the loaminess of the soil, and the tang of the aliens' blood as it soaked into it, making my nose twitch. My sense of smell had faded since the fever had left me, but the aromas above ground were pungent, and I could smell the thick undergrowth of the jungle circling the clearing.

The blue trees that had been so vivid in the day were now silhouetted black in the light from the other moons, and they loomed over us like sleeping giants. The command center and supply building were both low, flat-roofed structures with dull metal exteriors and no visible windows. Thin antennae and spires extended from the top, reaching spindly fingers toward the stars and sending out invisible signals.

I spotted no more guards near the command center, releasing a small breath of relief as I glanced back at the group. I locked my gaze on Lia, and she smiled at me. She was an experienced enough security officer that the quick killing of the Xulonians hadn't startled her, and she stepped over the bodies as if they were bothersome branches.

With a jerk of my head, I beckoned for the others to follow me, and we jogged to the door of the command center. As I'd thought, there were no visible security cameras. They didn't fear the unarmed creatures they dropped on the moon. Why should they? The well-armed hunters slaughtered their prey before they could even figure out what was going on or that there was a central command center. Not that anything like that would occur to the pursued creatures as they were running from hunters with sharp arrows and the ability to regenerate.

I scanned the large metal door and the panel next to it. There was no pad with symbols or numbers, only a smooth black surface smudged with fingerprints.

"A biometric scanner," Lia whispered. "I can't believe they use something so basic."

As a witness to the Xulonians advanced technology when they'd torn through the Taori shields and destroyed my ship, I knew they could have used something much more sophisticated. But there was no need here, I thought as a cold fury gathered inside me.

Walking back to the bodies we'd dragged inside the storage building, I swiftly hacked off one of the alien's hands. I returned to the door and pressed the disembodied palm to the scanner. The pad hummed to life, a green light glowing around the hand before the door clicked open.

"Aren't you glad we didn't set the bodies on fire?" Baboo whispered to Rafe.

Rafe cut his eyes to the spike-headed alien but didn't answer.

Yara, who'd been quiet up until that moment, cleared her

throat. "I'll stand guard outside, in case any soldiers or dimensional incarnations return."

"Are you sure?" Lia swept her gaze across the edge of the jungle. "You don't have a weapon."

"Don't worry about Yar." Rafe winked at the alien with white hair that almost shone silver in the moonlight. "She's not unarmed."

Yara smiled sweetly and held up her hands encased in black, gossamer gloves. "My skin is poisonous to the touch. Not much of a help when you're being shot at, but handy up close."

"I will stay with her," Baboo said. "In case the enemy doesn't come close enough to touch."

I gave both a curt nod. "Show no mercy."

"Don't worry." Yara's smile vanished. "I won't."

The alien who spoke only in clicks said something to Yara that made her laugh, then we left the pair stationed outside. As we slipped into the command center and stood in a gunmetal-gray hallway with ambient blue light coming from the floor, the sounds and smells of the outside world disappeared. For a command hub, it was surprisingly quiet, with only the hum of the lights and the muffled buzz of static in the distance.

I checked that Lia was behind me and motioned for Rafe to extinguish his flames. The fire starter frowned but complied. We'd made it this far without tripping any security alarms. I didn't want the enemy to have any indication that they were about to be slaughtered.

We moved in a tight formation down the corridor, not even our feet making noise as we all walked on our toes. As glad as I was that we hadn't been seen yet, the quiet of the alien hub unnerved me. Was it normal for a command center to be nearly deserted? The presence of the guards outside was proof that there were indeed others inside, but where was everyone?

We reached a door and a long clear panel that extended to

the side of it. Pausing, I peered cautiously around the door frame and through the glass. I'd hoped to see some sort of communications systems—consoles connected to the antennae outside, and possibly Xulonians manning them. Since our first order of business was to take out the comms systems so the command center couldn't call for help or reinforcements, we needed to locate those transmitters.

The machines behind the long glass were not transmitters. My skin prickled with revulsion when I realized that I was looking at rows of standing pods filled with Xulonian avatars. With shiny, red skin pulled tight over angular faces, the bodies were hooked into cylindrical pods as they regenerated and awaited the next occupant.

My heart raced, and my fingers tightened around my blade. Next to taking out the comms, destroying the avatars and the pods that kept them reanimating was at the top of our list. My rational officer's brain battled with my warrior's desire for revenge as my body thrummed with the need to punish the cowardly killers.

"Change of plans," I whispered to my crew.

FORTY-THREE

Lia

T he sight of so many sleeping aliens, their skin glowing red in the uplit pods, made cold fear slither down my spine. These were the aliens who'd chased me through the jungle, firing arrows intending to kill me, and all for a bit of entertainment.

The scent of antiseptic was powerful, and I took shallow breaths to keep from heaving as a wave of nausea overwhelmed me. I wondered which one of these replicas had fired the arrows that flew over my head. Which one had shot the arrow that lodged in Torst's arm?

I swallowed, a bitter tang rising at the back of my throat. "Now we know where to come once we've disabled the comms."

"Like I said," Torst growled, spinning the hilt of his blade in his hand. "Change of plans. We kill them now."

"But what if they're hooked up to some sort of scanners or monitors?" I whispered, looking from Torst to the others for support. "What if taking them out triggers an alarm, and we can't get to the communications hub in time? Then our attack is ruined. The Xulonians will send in reinforcements, and any ship that attempts to leave the moon will be blown from the sky."

The other survivors shifted nervously as they looked from me to Torst.

He met my gaze, his eyes blazing with rage. "These are the monsters who tried to kill all of us. They aren't even alive. They're only husks that are filled with whichever cowardly Xulonian pays enough for the pleasure to hunt down innocents. Destroying them won't even be killing, but it will eliminate their ability to hunt us again."

"He's right." Rafe flicked a small ball of fire into existence in his palm. "We take these out, and we take out their hold over the planet. Let's see them hunt us down if they actually have to send soldiers to risk their own lives."

I glanced over my shoulder at the door, hoping we hadn't been detected but aware that each passing second upped our chances of being caught. "Let's stick to the plan. Take out the comms and then take out the avatars."

The lights at the base of each of the pods pulsed crimson, casting a red hue over all of us, and making Torst's face look almost demonic as he glowered at me. "Plans change on the battlefield, Lia."

"This isn't a battlefield. It's a stealth attack that isn't going to be stealth for much longer."

Torst's blue eyes were almost entirely black, and I was reminded of how he'd looked at me when he was in the deepest throes of the mating fever. His gaze was just as molten hot, but this time it was fury I read and not desire.

"If you don't want to join me, don't, but I'm going to do

what has to be done." With that, he opened the first pod and sliced off the avatar's head with a single slash across the spindly throat. Blue blood spurted out and then gurgled down the front of the avatar's purple uniform.

Revulsion made my throat thick as I looked away. The avatars might not be real, but they were undoubtably organic and modeled to appear as genuine as possible.

Rafe rushed forward as Torst opened another pod, wrenching open one of the clear doors and setting the avatar inside on fire. He slammed the door shut to contain the blaze, watching with undisguised pleasure as the creature burned until all the oxygen was gone. The blackened hull that remained looked nothing like the scarlet creature it had once been.

I'd seen Torst in action before. He'd attacked like a predator when he'd defended me from the hunters, his skills as a fighter overpowering them even when they were armed, and he wasn't. But watching him move from pod to pod beheading the avatars wasn't like watching a battle. It was like witnessing an execution. As his chest heaved and his tail swished from side to side, I wondered if he was truly cured from the fever or if there were lingering effects making him so bloodthirsty.

Or maybe you don't know him like you think you do, a small voice in the back of my brain whispered to me. Maybe he's more of a beast than he can admit, or you can allow yourself to see.

Even as blood splattered the floor, I forced myself to reject this thought. Torst was only defending himself and all of us from an alien race so callous and violent that they believed slavery and murder were entertainment. Did the Xulonians deserve any mercy, and did Torst deserve my doubt?

The scent of burning flesh filled the air despite Rafe sealing every scorched body inside their pods, and I backed up with my hand over my nose. "Now can we complete our mission?"

Torst turned from decapitating the last avatar, his face

speckled with blue and his eyes wild. "Lead on, imperial soldier."

I bristled at this. "What does that mean?"

Rafe cut his eyes to Torst, the wicked grin on his face widening. "I told him about the empire you work for, that's all."

Torst drew in a breath and squared his shoulders, his tail slowing its fast twitching and the blue returning to his eyes. "I meant nothing. We should continue to the comms hub."

I swung my gaze to Rafe. The alien had always struck me as mischievous, but now I wondered if he was more dangerous than that. "What about the empire?"

Rafe twitched one shoulder as if he didn't have a care in the world. As if he hadn't just set a bunch of bodies on fire. "Your Taori is new to our time and space. He didn't understand that the empire will not be coming to rescue you. Not when they allow Xulon to operate with impunity."

His words were like a punch to the gut. "That isn't true. If the empire knew about this, they would act."

Rafe laughed low, the mirth in it dissipating almost instantly. "The empire acts in its own interests, like every empire before it. You truly believe they don't know about the slavers and the mercenaries? You don't think they get tribute for their ability to ignore what Xulon does?" He shook his head at me. "I know you aren't as naïve as you look, pretty human."

Anger flared in me. I'd gone to the imperial military academy. I'd had their code of honor and duty drummed into me. I'd diligently represented the empire as a security officer. I refused to believe they knew any of this or that I'd been a clueless pawn. "You don't know what you're talking about. The empire would never conspire with the Xulonians or take tribute to keep quiet. They would never stoop so low as to associate with such vile cowards."

"I'm afraid you're wrong about that, human," a voice said from behind us, "although I do object to being called a vile coward."

We all spun around to see a tall Xulonian step into the room with a blaster in his hand.

CHAPTER
FORTY-FOUR

Torst

I clenched my fists by my side as cold malice filled me. The alien wasn't like the ones I'd just dispatched. He wasn't wearing a blue or purple form-fitting suit that would blend into the jungle as he hunted. He wore long gray robes that covered everything but his bony hands and his crimson face, the eyes stark white and narrowed into slits as he leveled his weapon at me.

"This is unexpected." He flicked his gaze over our group. "I had no idea there were so many of our prey running loose." His lipless mouth curled. "How convenient of you to come here together. Saves our citizens the trouble of hunting you down."

I stole a glance at Lia, edging my way toward her. She had no weapon, and I had to protect her. If I'd thought she might appear scared or rattled by the enemy, I was wrong. Her face was set in a mask of disdain and fury that made me proud. There would be no cowering or crying from her.

"Your citizens aren't going to be hunting anyone for a while," Rafe said, his hands behind his back to hide the two balls of fire swirling in his palms.

The Xulonian shifted his gaze to the pods behind us, his expression freezing for a beat before his pronounced jaw clenched. Then he slid his gaze to me. "You must be the reason for all this trouble." He cocked his head to one side, his hood slipping down to reveal a bald, shiny skull. "What are you?"

I didn't want to give this creature any more of an advantage than he already had, but I intended to kill him, so what did it matter if he knew my name?

"Torst of the Immortal Army of the Taori."

"The Taori, yes," the alien said. "Didn't we destroy your ship when you encroached on our sovereign territory?"

Memories of the exploding sky ship made my fingers prickle with a rage that would only be quenched when I could wrap my hands around the Xulonian's neck and squeeze the life from him. My answer was a low growl as I adjusted the grip of my blade, the blood of his avatars still clinging to the sharp edge.

Not only did I want to kill this creature and every one of his entitled kinsmen who had engaged in enslaving other species and hunting them down like beasts, but I wanted to fall on my own blade for letting us end up at his mercy. Lia had been right. We should have taken out the communications systems before unloading our vengeance on the inanimate avatars. Maybe if we'd followed our plan, the Xulonian wouldn't be holding us at blaster point, and our attack wouldn't be in jeopardy of falling apart.

I'd been bent on revenge for so long—first against the Sythians for taking Kaolin from me and now against these Xulonians for threatening Lia and hunting me—that I didn't know how to exist without being fueled by rage. Vengeance had been my faithful companion for so long, I found it painful to release it and embrace another path. Even if the other path led to something better.

I glanced at Lia again. How had I let my vendetta take over my training? My clever mate had been right, and I'd risked all of us in my thirst for blood.

"I'm surprised our mercenaries didn't find you." The Xulonian's voice was as calm as if we were exchanging pleasantries. "They were highly recommended by the empire."

Lia flinched noticeably, and the alien smiled at her.

"I'm sorry to say that your friend is right about your precious empire. They know all about our moons and are paid handsomely to look the other way. Not that it is anyone's concern how my people entertain themselves."

"It is if you abduct other species and murder them," Lia snapped. "My imperial transport didn't enter your sovereign territory. We were attacked by slavers and brought to you."

The red-skulled alien raised one shoulder. "If we're offered merchandise, is it our duty to determine how it was sourced?"

"Yes! It's against the imperial code to harm a transport or the officers on it." Lia glared at him. "Maybe you've gotten away with taking humans from pleasure cruisers before, but you'll pay for what you've done to my imperial transport. The empire *will* search for us."

A weary sigh from the Xulonian. "You're correct about one thing. It will cost us more to smooth over the acquisition of so many humans from the empire, but you're wrong about the empire searching for you." He dropped his voice to a conspiratorial hiss. "No one is coming to save you."

Lia jerked back, her eyes widening. I wasn't sad that she'd learned the truth of the empire she worked for, but I hated the pain and betrayal etched on her face. Her shoulders sagged as if some of the fight had been drained from her, and her gaze dropped to the floor.

"That's the problem with empires," Rafe said. "They're all the same no matter how many centuries pass or how many wars are fought. None of you ever learn the truth about subjugating others to your will."

"What is that truth?" The alien swung his blaster so that it pointed at Rafe.

Rafe rolled the flaming orbs in is hands behind him. "That we always rise up and burn it all to the ground."

The Xulonian's finger curled around the trigger, a menacing grin slowly splitting his face. Then Rafe whipped his hands around, and the alien's eyes flew wide as a ball of flames was hurled toward him.

The alien fired wildly as he dodged to one side, and Rafe dove for the floor before he could release the second fire ball. The Xulonian unleashed a spray of blaster fire as he stumbled forward. He was as bad a shot as the hunting avatars, but the alien who spoke in clicks dropped like a stone, the scattered blaster fire hitting him. I lunged for Lia.

Before I could reach her and pull her down, a red hand snaked around her neck and jerked her up and flush to him, the point of the enemy's blaster pressing hard against her side. "If you want her, you'll have to follow her back into the jungle. If any one of you does not follow us outside, the female will die."

Rafe stood with a ball of flame at the ready, but there was no way to throw it at the Xulonian without risking burning Lia. I reached out and put a warning hand on his arm, and he lowered his hand with a growl that was as guttural as any of mine.

My stomach sank as Lia was dragged backward from the room. The cowardly alien was luring us from the building using Lia as bait. Before she disappeared down the corridor, she locked eyes with me and mouthed "Comms."

"Did she just say what I think she did?" Rafe asked once we were alone in the room. "What do we do?"

I thought of Lia and how tightly my soul was entwined with hers. I could not survive losing her, even if it meant certain death by remaining on the moon. I glanced at the dead alien sprawled on the floor and wondered if he was only the first of our group to perish. "We ignore her."

CHAPTER
FORTY-FIVE

Lia

The blaster jabbed into my side and the hard metal made me flinch as the Xulonian yanked me from the room and dragged me down the corridor toward the exit.

"Let's see how long it takes your friends to join you again in the hunt," he said, his voice thin between breaths. "You might have taken out my dimensional incarnations, but there are still two teams of mercenaries out there."

I didn't respond, my mind too busy whirring with possibilities. Could I grab the blaster and turn the tables on the alien before he fired off a shot? Could I somehow warn Yara and Baboo before we emerged from the building? Could I stall him and buy some time for Torst and the others to find and disable the communications systems?

I had no reason to believe that the Xulonian was lying about killing me if the others didn't come outside, but I hoped they would defy him anyway. Since there weren't alarms sounding in the building, I suspected he hadn't been able to alert anyone else because he'd genuinely been surprised to find us. Maybe he intended to take care of us himself so no one else would know that the building had been breached and the avatars destroyed.

That thought gave me a sliver of hope. If he was trying to keep this quiet to cover up his own failing in letting a bunch of their prey attack the command center, maybe I could use that to my advantage. At the very least, I didn't need to worry about being swarmed with more Xulonians brandishing blasters.

My gaze was trained on the doorway we'd just exited, but no one emerged. I ached to see Torst again, but I also didn't want him anywhere near the Xulonian holding me captive. Knowing the Taori, I couldn't trust him not to sacrifice himself to free me, when what I really wanted him to do was carry out the original plan.

Disable the communications, I thought, wishing the Taori counted mind reading among their abilities.

We reached the door and the Xulonian leaned hard against it, causing the latch to spring and a blast of thick air to hit us as the metal door swung open.

"Your plan to kill us all isn't going to work," I said hurriedly, hoping Yara and Baboo would hear my warning and hide.

"Why not? This moon was designed to kill you."

I was jerked outside and pushed hard toward the tree line of the jungle, the leafy fronds swaying toward me in the breeze like hungry, grasping arms. Stumbling and bracing myself with my hands, I crouched on the ground and peered up at the alien. His long robes fluttered as he stood silhouetted in the moonlight with his arms extended and the blaster aimed at me.

"You're not really going to let me go back into the jungle, are you?" I asked.

He twitched one shoulder. "This is a hunting moon. Each

creature we bring to the hunt is an expense. If I kill all our prey, I'll have to explain to the praetor why I require a new shipment."

"But you don't have any more hunters."

His red face contorted for a moment, making him look ever more the monster in the shadowy light. "Our dimensionals can be repaired, although it might take a while."

"So, you'd rather the mercenaries kill us?"

"I only need the mercenaries to kill one of you." He shifted the blaster in his hand, the shiny skin stretched tight across sharp knuckles. "Or maybe I'll save them the trouble and shoot him myself. The mercenaries can hunt the rest of you, wearing you down to make you easier prey for when our citizens return to the hunt."

My stomach churned with the knowledge that the "one" he was talking about was Torst. I stole a glance at the door, my pulse spiking. I couldn't let him kill Torst. Not after everything he'd done to save me. Not after everything we'd shared, and what he meant to me.

As much as I teased him about being a sweet talker, I believed him when he said his soul was bound to mine. Our connection was more than just physical, and it had morphed from me helping cure his mating fever to our bodies being locked to each other in more ways than one. I'd never experienced such a complete sense of belonging to another being. I might not have been one to believe in fate or true love or soul mates, but there was no doubt in my mind that I was forever bound to the Taori. As stubbornly independent as I'd been my entire life, the idea of being his mate didn't even make me flinch.

I couldn't even be mad that he'd killed all the avatars first. He'd been right about the empire, and I'd been a fool to think that imperial power wouldn't crave money over honor.

A shadow slipped from behind the side of the building behind the Xulonian and moved silently toward us. Yara! My heart leapt at the willowy silhouette then instantly stuttered in my chest. The angle of the moons cast her shadow forward, which meant that soon the Xulonian would see her approach.

I took a few steps back toward the command center door to get the moons behind me, spreading my arms wide and motioning to the jungle. "Have you ever been out there on the hunt?"

His blaster tracked me as he shook his head. "Only elite citizens can afford the Moorla moons, but the hunt doesn't interest me."

I gave him a knowing smile. "The lust moon then?"

His skin was so red I wouldn't have known if he'd flushed, but his eyes darted down my body, and he licked his thin lips. "A female like you was wasted on this moon."

I fought a wave of revulsion, steeling my expression so he wouldn't see my disgust or notice that I was watching Yara approach from the corner of my eye. "Why don't you take me to the other moon? You're in charge, aren't you? You could do that."

His eyes widened, but he shook his head. "No one makes those calls but the praetor. You have to stay here until the hunters kill you."

"Too bad," I said, stepping nearly in front of the door and holding my breath as Yara crept ever closer to the alien, quietly slipping off her gloves.

The Xulonian cut his gaze to the door behind me, his top lip curling. "Time's up for your friends. It looks like the hunters won't be the ones to kill you after all."

As his finger closed around the trigger, the blaster spun from his hand. He yelped in surprise, so startled by being disarmed by an invisible force that the Xulonian didn't notice as

Yara wrapped her hands around his neck from behind. Before the blaster hit the ground, the alien let out a shriek of pain. Yara didn't release her grip as he sank to his knees, his arms still waving as blaster fire sprayed into the air when the weapon finally landed. Behind me, the door flew open, and Torst rushed forward, with Rafe flanking him.

They both skidded to a stop when they spotted the alien writhing on the ground, as Yara held her poisonous hands to his flesh. Baboo rushed from around the side of the command center, releasing a squeak as the Xulonian's face melted into the dirt, and Rafe lowered his flaming hands with a sigh.

"You got to have all the fun, Yar."

She stood and tugged her gloves back on, giving Rafe a sweet smile. "You were late."

Torst turned to me, relief evident on his face as he put his hands on my waist and pinned me with an intense gaze. "My need for vengeance put you in danger. It will never happen again."

I smiled up at him, my head swimming for a moment as my legs wobbled. Then Torst pulled back a hand from my waist, his large palm almost black in the dim light as it dripped with blood. The warmth in my side enveloped my entire body, and he caught me as I sank to the ground.

CHAPTER
FORTY-SIX

Torst

L ia's body was light in mine as I dropped to the ground, cradling her in my arms. My throat closed, trapping the roar that ached to burst from me. Her blood was warm and sticky on my hands, as I pressed it to the blaster wound on her side. I was vaguely aware of voices around me—Baboo's hysterical one and Rafe's anger-laced one—but the sounds melded into a low hum behind the noise of blood rushing in my ears.

Finally, Yara's voice cut through them all as she knelt next to me. "We need to get her to Zennen. We'll be able to heal her with his potions."

I pushed aside the grief that was choking me as I stared down at Lia's face, her lips colorless and her eyelids still. "She won't survive being carried down the ladder and all that way."

Yara stood. "Then I'll get Zennen and bring him to her."

"Hurry," I whispered to her retreating form as she disappeared into the storage building.

"I'm going back in." Rafe's hands were fists by his side, sparks shooting from between the tightly clenched fingers. "We still need to destroy the communications systems, before those assholes realize one of their crew is missing." He cut a pained gaze to Lia. "It's what we should have done first, like she said."

I gave him a solemn nod. He was right. I wished I could go with him, but I wouldn't leave Lia. It was my fault she was fighting for her life, and I'd never be able to live with myself if I left her now. Not even if it meant the mission failed.

Guilt slammed into me that I'd let our plan fall apart. If I'd listened to her and we'd taken out the comms first, the Xulonian might not have found us and taken Lia hostage. Then I gritted my teeth as my resolve hardened into certainty. I would not allow Lia to pass beyond the veil to the shadowland. I pressed my hand to her, sending my life force energy into her and banishing death's seductive whispers.

"Our fate was written in the stars," I murmured to her, stroking a finger down the side of her face. "Our story does not end here."

No more, I thought as I held her small body against mine. No matter what happened to our mission, I would no longer allow my life to be governed by my quest for vengeance. It ended now. I'd found my true mate in Lia. Pain and revenge had no more place in my heart.

"Do you hear that?"

I peered up at Baboo as he stood beside me gazing toward the jungle. Even in the shadowy darkness, his face was pinched with worry. I stilled my breathing as I listened, fear chilling my skin at the rustling of branches and crunching of undergrowth. Those were not the sounds of animals. The mercenaries had found us. I wished Rafe hadn't gone inside the command center, even though the communications needed to be destroyed. His fire balls would have come in handy against a team of trained killers, but I'd also faced worse odds.

"Can I trust you with my mate?" I asked Baboo.

He bobbed his head earnestly as he knelt next to me. "I waited too late to take the blaster from the alien. This is my fault."

"It is no one's fault but the Xulonian who took her, but you can keep her alive for me, my friend. Keep pressure on her wound." I reluctantly removed my hand from her and reached for my blade. "I'll take care of what's coming for us."

Baboo held his trembling hand to Lia's side, hunching over her so that her body was shielded with his.

I stood and rested a hand on his shoulder. "Courage is not the absence of fear. It is the strength to ride into the valley of death despite the terror." He looked up at me, meeting my gaze with a determined look on his face, and I squeezed his shoulder. "I ride beside you proudly, friend."

I rushed forward, my tail thrashing as the figures burst from the jungle. Leaping into the air, I came down on top of the first soldier and drove my blade into his throat. With a gurgling cry, he collapsed, and I scooped his laser rifle from the ground. I spun and fired at the other soldiers as they advanced on me. Red blasts of laser fire shot from their weapons, and I dove into the jungle, the heat of the laser skimming over my back.

The air was filled with yells as the mercenaries regrouped, trying to locate me in the dark. I could easily see them swinging their weapons in wide arcs, and I tossed a stick away from me to draw their fire. They pivoted to the sound and unleashed their rifles, allowing me time to run through the jungle to one side.

It only took them a moment to realize that I'd tricked them.

"He's over there!"

"Forget him. Go for the ones over there!"

My heart plummeted as I saw two of the fighters pivot to where Baboo hunched on the ground shielding Lia. But as they ran toward him, the door to the storage building tore off its hinges and flew at them, knocking them off their feet and pinning them beneath it.

The other mercenaries staggered back, scanning the area for who'd done that, but I knew it had been Baboo. His face was intense with concentration, his eyes glittering in the moonlight. A warrior worthy of being an Immortal, I thought.

Surging forward with my head down and my horns as a battering ram, I took two of the fighters by surprise and slammed them to the ground before unleashing a barrage of laser fire into their backs. As the remaining mercenaries turned on me, I dashed back into the jungle and crouched behind a copse of spindly trees that barely shielded me from the torrent of weapons fire.

I gathered a breath as the fighters advanced on me. I would need to rush them before they could turn on Baboo and Lia again. Despite his abilities, the little alien couldn't hold them off by himself, and I suspected that ripping a steel door off its hinges had taken a great deal of his powers.

As I prepared to charge at the mercenaries, I was startled by a bellow that didn't come from them. I knew the guttural sound of the war cry that rent the air as a hulking figure joined the battle, his silvery horns catching in the light.

CHAPTER
FORTY-SEVEN

Torst

Daiken barreled forward, his snarls nearly as loud as the mercenaries' screams as he rammed them with his horns before slashing at their prone bodies with his blade. I joined the fray, driving my own blade into the attacking fighters until it was slick with blood. When the bodies of the enemy were lifeless on the ground, my Taori shipmate and I stood shoulder to shoulder heaving in ragged breaths.

"Into the valley of death," I said, swiping my dripping blade clean on my pants and stealing a glance at his wild eyes and swishing tail. He was so deep in the grip of the fever I wasn't sure if he'd heard me.

"Rode the Ten Thousand," he finally said in a strangled voice, before staggering away through the jungle.

"Daiken!" I called after him. My heart ached at how the Quaibyn was ravaging him, but there was still a shadow of the warrior I knew beneath the primal urges and carnal desires. If I could get him off the moon and to a civilized planet—or even find enough sedation—I could save him.

"Torst." Baboo's weak voice brought me back to the carnage.

Spinning toward him, I limped over to where he pressed his hands to Lia's wound, although his shoulders sagged. It was clear how much effort it had taken to tear the door off the building and stop the mercenaries.

I sank to the ground beside him, placing my hands over his. "I owe you a debt of a thousand lifetimes, friend."

He managed a weak smile. "One will do just fine."

Rafe burst from the command center behind us, his arms outstretched with flaming orbs in each hand ready to be hurled. He skidded to a stop when he saw the mercenaries scattered on the ground and the metal door lying on top of two of them. Then his gaze went to us, and Lia sprawled pale and motionless on the ground.

He doused his flaming hands and knelt beside me. "The communications systems are destroyed, along with any Xulonian who would have been able to send out a message."

I nodded, my throat too tight to speak. Lia's face was drained of all color, and her chest barely rose and fell anymore. Had we succeeded in our mission only to lose her? I shook my head, refusing to believe that.

I bent over her so that my lips feathered the soft shell of her ear. "I do not release you to the shadowland. I am bound to your heart, and my soul is yours. Where you go, I go. We do not follow the seductive whispers of Death this night." My voice cracked. "Do you hear me, little one? It is my voice that beckons you with sweet promises. Not Death's. He will not claim your soul." I peered up defiantly into the sky. "Unless he intends to take mine as well."

I was only vaguely aware of Rafe's hand on my shoulder and

Baboo's hands beneath mine before Zennen was pushing me aside and bending over Lia.

I fell back, my hands coated with her blood as he assessed her wound and muttered to himself before digging a small bottle from inside a fabric satchel and tipping the contents into Lia's mouth.

"I can save her," the willowy alien said with a sigh. "She will live."

Many hands pulled me to my feet, as well as Baboo and Rafe. All the survivors were there, along with Val, who slapped a hand over her mouth when she saw Lia.

As Val huddled with Zennen and Yara over Lia, Rafe cleared his throat. "We should get off the moon before the home world attempts contact and realizes something is wrong."

The fire starter was right. Now that I knew Lia would live, I released a breath. "Or the second mercenary team finds us."

A rumble passed through the group and nervous glances were exchanged.

Zennen twisted his neck around, his gaze meeting mine. "The faster we get Lia onto a ship and stabilized, the better."

"The shipyard is behind the command center." Rafe jerked a thumb over his shoulder as he backed toward it.

"Can she be moved?" I asked Zennen as he stood. Already, there was color back in Lia's face, and her chest rose and fell in an even cadence.

"I will move her," Baboo said, his brow furrowing as he stared hard at Lia until her body lifted off the ground. She levitated at his chest level as he followed Rafe toward the ship.

The entire group of survivors shuffled behind Rafe, Baboo, and Lia as we moved around the low command center. My heart thumped in anticipation as the silver sky ship came into view. It wasn't a battleship, but it was larger than a fighter or shuttle, with a shiny hull that gleamed in the light from the other moons. This must be one of the ships that transported staff from Xulon to work in the command center because it looked large enough to hold sleeping quarters. Which meant there was probably a medical bay with supplies.

I caught up to Zennen and Val, who were walking together. "Thank you for saving her."

Zennen inclined his head at me. "Thank you for making it possible for us to escape."

"We aren't free from the enemy's grasp yet," I warned him.

He rested thin fingers on my arm. "You have given us all the taste of freedom. We are already free." He nodded at me with a small smile as I glanced at Lia's levitating body being walked up hovering steps of light into the belly of the ship. "Now go join your mate."

I gave a final glance back at the alien moon, my gut twisting that my Taori brother had chosen to stay behind. He'd saved me —all of us, really—but I hadn't been able to save him. Then I let my gaze rest on Lia, her eyelids fluttering with life again. My priority was saving her. I would spill tears for the sacrifice of my fellow Taori later.

CHAPTER
FORTY-EIGHT

Lia

Torst's face slowly came into focus. His brow was creased, and blood was smeared on his cheeks and horns.

He gently put a calloused hand to my cheek. "Don't try to talk."

"She isn't an invalid." Zennen appeared at Torst's side, smiling and shaking his head as his antennae bobbled. "I believe the female has proven how tough she is already. A blaster wasn't going to bring her down."

Torst frowned at this. "She never should have been in the path of that alien's blaster."

I blinked at the bright lights shining overhead and the gleaming white ceiling, ignoring the argument brewing. We weren't in the tunnels or in the command center. The slight antiseptic smell reminded me of the many medical bays I'd been in, my body instantly tensing at the childhood memories of needle pricks and foul-tasting medicines. "Where am I?"

Torst took my hand in his, the solid feel of his much larger hand grounding me. "On a sky ship heading away from the moon."

Thoughts raced through my head. The last thing I remembered was being dragged from the command center by the Xulonian, and then watching as Baboo disarmed him and Yara killed him with her poisonous hands. After that, all I could summon was a vague mash-up of screams, blaster fire, and terrifying growls. "Yara—"

"Is here on the ship," Zennen said. "We all are. Your boyfriend and the rest of your attack team managed to do it."

I glanced to Torst for confirmation, and he nodded. "The communications were taken out and all the Xulonians killed. We dispatched one mercenary team before taking the sky ship off the moon."

I slowly sat up, propping myself on my elbows. "How far are we from Xulon?"

Rafe poked his head inside the small room. "I can answer that." He winked at me. "Good to see you up again, Lia. We're free from the moon's orbit, and headed for the nearest moon to fly behind for cover before we leave Xulonian space."

"We thought it would be wise to attract as little attention as possible from Xulon," Zennen said, "although they will figure out what happened on their hunting moon eventually."

"But we'll be long gone by then," Rafe said. "Once we hit imperial territory, we plan to send a transmission notifying the empire of your abduction."

"And my crew." My chest constricted at the thought of my dead colleagues and the other women still on the other moons. "We can't leave without the rest of them." I pinned Torst with a pointed look. "And what about the other stranded Taori? We can't leave them to the cruelty of the Xulonians."

Rafe rubbed his hands together, sparks flying from between his fingers. "If that means taking out more red skulls, you can count on me."

Torst grunted. "First, we need to gather reinforcements and weapons."

Rafe muttered something as he shrugged. "Let's hope the empire shows some honor."

I'd lost faith in the imperial power I'd been so loyal to, but I also knew that they would not want to lose face or be seen as dishonorable. "I'll get them on our side." Then I remembered the shipmate I'd been stranded with. "Where's Val?"

Rafe tilted his head to one side. "She was with us getting on the ship, but I'm not sure where she is now. If you want to see her, I can go find her."

I nodded, eager to talk to my one link to the old ship, even though that life now seemed like ages ago. Rafe gave me another mischievous wink and disappeared.

"Now that we know it's possible to beat the Xulonians and escape, we have to free the other moons," I said.

"And tell the universe of the crimes of the Xulonians," Zennen added, bitterly. "They must pay for enslaving and murdering innocents."

"First, Lia must recuperate." Torst stepped closer to me. "There will be plenty of chances for you to be reckless again."

I gasped. "Reckless? Me?" Before I could launch into a diatribe about how reckless he'd been, I noticed the smile teasing the corner of his mouth. I swatted at him as he pulled me into his chest and wrapped his arms around me fiercely.

Zennen slipped from the room, leaving us alone as Torst hitched in a breath.

"I thought I'd lost you to the shadowland."

I sank into the warmth of his big body, rubbing a hand down the smooth hardness of his chest, as he curled his tail around my back. "If I didn't leave you to drown in the sea, I wasn't going to leave you just because of a little blaster hit."

A gravelly laugh rumbled through him. "For once, I'm grateful my mate is such a stubborn female."

My cheeks warmed. Between the mating fever and being forced into one adrenaline-fueled and dangerous situation after another, there had been lingering doubt in the back of my mind as to whether Torst would feel the same way about us once we were safe. "Your mate?"

He pulled back from me. "You're my mate, Lia. If teasing death cannot break our bond, nothing can." A crease formed between his eyes. "Do you regret binding yourself to me, little one?"

I shook my head, tears shocking me by springing to my eyes. "I don't regret anything. Not even being taken by slavers and dumped onto the hunting moon. If it brought me to you, it was worth it."

Torst cupped my chin in his hand and tipped my face up to meet his. "I would battle ten thousand red skulls, if you were on the other end of the battlefield."

Then he crushed his mouth to mine, parting my lips in a claiming kiss that sent jolts of desire through me. My recovery was forgotten as I wrapped my arms around his neck and surrendered to his devouring kiss. When he tore his lips from mine, his eyes flashed molten—a reminder that the feverish Taori who'd been nearly mad with lust still lurked within him.

"Remind me again," I whispered, grabbing both of his horns as I swung my legs off the platform bed so that they circled his waist. "How long until your next bout of mating fever?"

He growled and nipped at my neck, kicking the door behind us closed. "I believe I feel it coming on now."

EPILOGUE

Valeria woke up shivering, the cold seeping into her bones like a familiar ache. The fur beneath her cheek was scratchy and smelled like it had been wet. Another fur covered her shoulders, the weight of it making her head feel even heavier. She breathed in, surprised by the faint mineral scent clinging to the cool air.

Where was she?

Her temples throbbed as she tried to remember, but the last vision that drifted up to her brain was walking toward the alien ship behind Lia and Torst and the other alien survivors. Zennen had been beside her, but then he'd hurried ahead to help an injured Lia up the ship's hovering light steps. She could recall the thick, humid air of the jungle around them, and the sounds of the night—the chirping of insects and the faint caw of a bird as the dawn approached.

The looming, silver hull of the Xulonian ship had been a welcome sight, and her pulse had quickened as the engines had hummed to life and she'd gotten closer. She'd paused to sneak a final glance at the strange jungle they'd escaped. Then everything had gone black. She had no memories of entering the ship or taking off. No memories of leaving the hunting moon.

Sitting up, Val moaned as she took in the dimly lit cavern, an iridescent, blue-green stream running along a crevice in the stone floor and disappearing through an opening in the rock, steam hovering over the surface. The flowing water provided the only light, casting an eerie glow on the walls that undulated like waves.

These weren't the tunnels she'd been in. For one, it was significantly colder here, and the other tunnels hadn't had a water source. She eyed the stream that illuminated everything around her. She'd never seen water that glowed like that. But even with the sounds of the trickling water that cascaded somewhere below her, Val detected something else that made the back of her neck prickle.

She scanned the rest of the cavern, her breath catching in her throat when she spotted the creature crouched in the darkest nook. She didn't need to hear him speak to know that this was the same Taori who'd taken her to the tunnels before. He looked much like Torst, with silvery horns curling back around his ears; long, dark hair; and a fur-tipped tail that twitched behind him. Like his Taori shipmate, he wore only animal-skin pants, with his heavily muscled chest bare, aside from the dark tattoos covering almost every speck of skin. Unlike Torst, whose eyes were as blue as the glowing water, his eyes were all black pupils.

"Daiken?"

His only answer was a guttural rumble that reverberated off the stone and into her bones.

Panic fluttered in her chest. "Where are we?"

"Safe underground," he growled.

Val pushed off the fur. "What about the ship? I was escaping with the others. Where are they?"

He jerked his gaze away from her and grunted. "Gone."

She fought the urge to scream. "Gone? But that was my only way off—our only way off. Now we're stuck on this hunting moon until they kill us."

Daiken shook his head. "I will never let them kill you. They will never find us. The hunters don't like to come to this side of the moon."

Fear slid down my spine. "What side of the moon? Where have you taken me?"

He shuffled closer, still on his haunches. "To the far side of the moon that's covered in ice."

That explained why she was so cold. Val rubbed her hands briskly over her arms.

"You won't freeze," he continued, his voice raspy. "The tunnels under the ice are warmed with subterranean springs."

The sounds of flowing water surrounded her, and Val noticed that the stream running through the cavern was fed by a short waterfall emerging from the back wall. How deep and long did the springs run?

"This is crazy." She shook her head. "We can't live under here. We need to escape. Maybe the others will come back for us if we return to the alien command center."

Another growl filled the cavern. "No. They'll take you from me."

Val remembered what Torst had said about the Taori mating fever. "You're sick. You need to be treated."

He shook his head as if trying to shake loose his horns. "I only need you."

Her heart raced, fear making her mouth go dry. "You can't keep me here against my will."

His gaze snapped to her, the expression in his eyes anguished. "I've known you were mine since the moment I scented you," he husked, his eyes glittering through the shadows. "You were meant to be my mate. If I don't claim you, I will go mad."

Panic seized her, and she leapt up and staggered toward the opening in the cavern even though her head swam. Before she'd even reached it, he was on her, coiling a massive arm around her body and jerking her flush to him. He towered over her, encasing her body in his as she struggled fruitlessly against him.

"Running will only stoke my need to chase you." He rasped, his words sending tremors of both fear and unwanted desire skittering across her skin.

Val let out a whimper that was met with a low throaty rumble. The Taori tightened his grip on her waist, nuzzling his stubbly cheek against her neck and inhaling deeply. "I am trying to tame myself for you, but if you insist on running, I cannot promise the mating fever won't overtake me." He ran the tip of his tongue along the shell of her ear. "And if that happens, there will be nothing slow or gentle about it."

～

THANK YOU FOR READING SUBMIT!

Want to read more of Torst and Lia? Click below to get a bonus steamy epilogue to SUBMIT!

GET THE BONUS EPILOGUE

～

IF YOU LOVED this sci-fi romance, you'll love book two in the series, STALK!

I almost escaped from this twisted hunting moon, until a delirious Taori warrior snatched me away. Sure, he thought he was saving me from a menacing swarm that haunts his dark and tortured memories, but now I'm stuck with him on this deadly moon that's crawling with mercenaries hunting me for sport.

To have any shot at survival, I need to stay in the Taori's under-ground lair, which wouldn't be so bad if he wasn't burning with mating fever and eyeing me like I'm a tasty snack. Unfortunately, the longer he fights the urge, the more dangerous he becomes.

One-click STALK>

This book has been edited and proofed, but typos are like little gremlins that like to sneak in when we're not looking. If you spot a typo, please report it to: tana@tanastone.com
Thank you!!

ALSO BY TANA STONE

The Sky Clan of the Taori:

SUBMIT

STALK

SEDUCE

Inferno Force of the Drexian Warriors:

IGNITE (also available on AUDIO)

SCORCH

BURN

BLAZE

FLAME

The Tribute Brides of the Drexian Warriors Series:

TAMED (also available in AUDIO)

SEIZED (also available in AUDIO)

EXPOSED (also available in AUDIO)

RANSOMED (also available in AUDIO)

FORBIDDEN (also available in AUDIO)

BOUND (also available in AUDIO)

JINGLED (A Holiday Novella) (also in AUDIO)

CRAVED (also available in AUDIO)

STOLEN (also available in AUDIO)

SCARRED (also available in AUDIO)

The Barbarians of the Sand Planet Series:

BOUNTY (also available in AUDIO)

CAPTIVE (also available in AUDIO)

TORMENT (also available on AUDIO)

TRIBUTE (also available as AUDIO)

SAVAGE (also available in AUDIO)

CLAIM (also available on AUDIO)

CHERISH: A Holiday Baby Short

PRIZE (Coming in 2022)

Raider Warlords of the Vandar Series:

POSSESSED (also available in AUDIO)

PLUNDERED (also available in AUDIO)

PILLAGED (also available in AUDIO)

PURSUED (also available in AUDIO)

PUNISHED (also available on AUDIO)

PROVOKED (also available in AUDIO)

Alien Academy Series:

ROGUE (also available in AUDIO)

All the TANA STONE books available as audiobooks!

INFERNO FORCE OF THE DREXIAN WARRIORS:

IGNITE on AUDIBLE

RAIDER WARLORDS OF THE VANDAR:

POSSESSED on AUDIBLE

PLUNDERED on AUDIBLE